"There's something special about us. I felt it from the beginning," Emily said.

"So did I." Nash pressed his mouth against hers.

She returned the kiss, inching her hands up his throat. With her fingers laced behind his neck, she pulled him closer and he deepened the kiss.

Nash's body jerked, and he pulled away from her.

"I—I agree." She put a hand to her hot cheek. "Bad idea."

"Shh." He rose to his feet and turned toward the sliding door that led to their room.

"What is it?" She touched his back, straining her ears for Wyatt's cry.

Nash lunged forward and charged through the door.

With the adrenaline rushing through her system, Emily stumbled after him. She tripped over the sliding-door track and screamed as she saw Nash tackle a man hovering over Wyatt's crib.

CHAIN
OF CUSTODY

CAROL ERICSON

HARLEQUIN®
INTRIGUE®

ISBN-13: 978-1-335-13659-6

Chain of Custody

Copyright © 2020 by Carol Ericson

This edition published by arrangement with Harlequin Books S.A.

For questions and comments about the quality of this book, please contact us at CustomerService@Harlequin.com.

Harlequin Enterprises ULC
22 Adelaide St. West, 40th Floor
Toronto, Ontario M5H 4E3, Canada
www.Harlequin.com

Printed in U.S.A.

Carol Ericson is a bestselling, award-winning author of more than forty books. She has an eerie fascination for true-crime stories, a love of film noir and a weakness for reality TV, all of which fuel her imagination to create her own tales of murder, mayhem and mystery. To find out more about Carol and her current projects, please visit her website at www.carolericson.com, "where romance flirts with danger."

CAST OF CHARACTERS

Emily Lang—A fired cop trying to get her PI business off the ground, she takes a job keeping tabs on baby Wyatt, and when that baby leads her to the doorstep of a sexy border patrol agent, she's only too willing to conceal her dislike of babies and pose as a nanny to get close to Wyatt—and the agent.

Nash Dillon—When an old friend drops her baby off on this border patrol agent's porch with little explanation, he's thrilled to find a caring nanny—until he discovers his nanny is a PI with ulterior motives and a fiery temperament to match her red hair.

Wyatt Lemoin—This innocent baby is at the center of a tug-of-war involving petty criminals, drug dealers and child traffickers.

Jaycee Lemoin—Nash's old friend has gotten herself, and her baby, into big trouble but she could always count on Nash to help her out.

Brett Fillmore—Jaycee's boyfriend isn't above using a baby to save his own skin, but he crossed the wrong people this time.

Marcus Lanier—A Phoenix mover and shaker, Marcus hires Emily to follow a baby he claims is his own, but is he a concerned father or something more sinister?

Chapter One

Emily held her breath as the man with the gun leaned over the playpen and ran the butt of the weapon down the front of the baby's onesie.

"Cute kid." His lips stretched into a semblance of a smile. "He yours?"

Jaycee started forward and then stopped, licking her lips.

Emily whispered to herself, "C'mon, Jaycee. Do what you do best. Lie."

Flicking her fingers in the air, Jaycee said, "It's my roommate's. I'm making her move and take the brat with her."

The bigger, beefier man in the room, who clearly didn't need a weapon for intimidation, strolled toward the window and out of Emily's view. "You sure you don't know where your boyfriend is?"

"I told you. Brett and I broke up. I don't have a clue where that loser is."

Emily squinted and brought the phone with the video flickering across the display closer to her face. Was Jaycee telling the truth this time?

Emily's client, Marcus Lanier, was sure Jaycee planned to take their baby and run off with Brett Fillmore. If Brett were in trouble with these two guys, Jaycee wouldn't be likely to hand him over.

The big man skimmed a hand over his shaved head as he stepped back into the range of the camera Emily had set up in Jaycee's apartment—without her knowledge. Once Marcus had hired her to keep an eye on his baby, Emily's first step had been to install some electronic surveillance in Jaycee's apartment. She hadn't gotten much info in the five days she'd been tracking Jaycee—until now.

Marcus Lanier, a mover and shaker in Phoenix, had suspected Jaycee of hanging out with a sketchy crowd, and these guys with their guns and veiled threats definitely qualified. Marcus had feared for his baby's safety due to Jaycee's relationship with Brett Fillmore, a low-level druggie, but these two were next-level serious.

What did they want with Brett? If they thought he was the father of this baby, what would they be willing to do?

"Wh-what do you want with Brett, anyway?" Jaycee crossed her arms and wedged her back against the playpen, blocking the baby from the intruders.

The man holstered his gun. "Don't worry about it. If you hear from him, let him know he needs to call us."

Jaycee finally asked the question Emily was dying to know. "Who's us?"

The bigger guy, the one who hadn't drawn the weapon tucked in his waistband, straightened the sunglasses he hadn't bothered to remove inside. "How many people are looking for him?"

The other man snorted. "Tell him to call us—or else."

Knots tightened in Emily's gut. Had Jaycee noticed he glanced at the baby when he said that?

"If I happen to see him, which I doubt, I'll let him know a couple of guys with guns are looking for him." Jaycee tossed her dyed blond locks over her shoulder. "I'm sure he'll get right on it."

The man with the shaved head leveled a finger at her. "You forgot the 'or else' part—and no police, or we'll be looking for you, too."

"Me and the police don't get along so well." Jaycee shrugged. "I don't think I'll have any contact with Brett, but I'll tell him if I do."

Emily blew out a long breath when the two men finally left. She'd been worried about the baby, but Jaycee must've been terrified despite her nonchalant attitude.

As soon as the door closed behind the men, Jaycee sprang into action. She ran toward the hallway and stayed out of view for a good ten minutes. She reappeared, dragging a suitcase behind her with a diaper bag slung over her shoulder.

Emily's heart rattled in her chest. Jaycee planned to leave. She'd better take the car Emily had put a tracker on, because Emily had no intention of letting that baby—or her own fat paycheck—out of her sight.

With one eye on her phone, Emily packed a bag almost as quickly as Jaycee had. She didn't have to pack baby stuff, but she had her own bag of tricks she might need on the road. She had to be prepared for anything. Jaycee might even try to slip across the border.

When the red dot on her phone indicated Jaycee was on the move, Emily grabbed a bottle of water and a half-eaten sandwich from the fridge. Holding her cell in front of her, she tossed her bag into the trunk of her car and slid behind the wheel.

She lived near enough to Jaycee's neighborhood in south Phoenix to wait it out on the street in front of her own place until she could determine Jaycee's intent. When her cell phone showed Jaycee's car heading for the 10 South, she cranked on her engine and peeled away from the curb.

Following Jaycee, Emily kept her distance—not that Jaycee would recognize her or her nondescript silver hatchback, but she might be keeping an eye out for a tail…at least she should be.

Emily checked her own rearview mirror, scanning the freeway behind her. Had the goons who'd dropped in on Jaycee believed her about the baby not being hers? Maybe they believed her about Brett. If they trusted anything that woman said, they didn't know Jaycee Lemoin very well—at least if all of Marcus Lanier's stories about her were true.

A half a sandwich, a bottle of water and about an hour and a half later, Emily watched on her phone's display as Jaycee cruised past Tucson. She flexed her fingers on the steering wheel. Did this chick really intend to cross the border?

If she did, maybe Marcus should just let her go. Maybe Jaycee and the baby could keep safe by getting lost in Mexico. But Marcus didn't want to let Jaycee go, and he wanted to keep the baby safe *from* Jaycee.

Emily hadn't even informed her client of this second threat stalking his son, but it wouldn't surprise him.

Marcus knew all about the company Jaycee kept and her lifestyle, making him fear for the baby's safety. He'd hired Emily to watch out for the baby until he could prove his paternity and get his ducks in a row before making a move for custody.

This little excursion of Jaycee's would give Marcus even more ammunition.

Emily's gaze darted to her phone and the red dot heading west. Did Jaycee plan to spend the night somewhere before crossing over? Or was she waiting for nightfall before making that surreptitious journey?

Five minutes later, Emily took the same exit—to Paradiso, a small Arizona border town.

Jaycee's car had stopped, and Emily blew out a breath. She could be a lot more inconspicuous in this little hick border town than in Mexico. If Jaycee decided to stay put in Paradiso, Emily would be able to watch her and the baby better. Then Marcus could take over and do whatever he needed to do to get his son back.

Emily sucked in her bottom lip when she turned off the main road running through the town. She'd expected Jaycee to hole up at a hotel. If she were staying with a friend, surveillance would be more difficult.

As she rolled past a grove of leafy trees, Emily buzzed down her window and sniffed the air, which had a slightly sweet smell. Who knew orchards grew in the middle of the desert?

She squinted and scanned the long, empty road ahead. Jaycee must've pulled into the gates on the right.

Nothing else but trees stretched on either side of the road. The house behind those gates must be set back from the street because Emily could see just the top of it.

Emily pulled into a turnoff well beyond the gates and dug in her bag for a pair of binoculars. She leaned out the car window and focused on the entrance to the property. She could research the records later for the owners and their connection to Jaycee.

She had barely settled in for her little watch party when Jaycee's car flew out of the gates, kicking up dust.

Emily pulled her head back in the car and tossed the binoculars onto the seat next to her. "Damn. On the road again."

She followed Jaycee into town and to a gas station on the edge of it. The woman hadn't made her once on the trip down and wouldn't take notice of another car fueling up.

After Jaycee got her gas, she walked into the mini-mart to pay, but she didn't have the baby with her. No wonder Marcus was concerned. That action right there screamed negligence. She'd add it to her list for Marcus's custody battle.

With her palms sweating, Emily scrambled from her car and strolled past Jaycee's at the pump. She glanced into the back seat of Jaycee's little compact and tripped, clutching a hand to her throat.

What had Jaycee done with the baby?

BORDER PATROL AGENT NASH DILLON logged off his computer and stretched his arms to the ceiling. It had been a rough few weeks after he'd come back from the rodeo in Wyoming. That headless body at the border before he'd left had ushered in a floodgate of information about a cartel's tunnels between the US and Mexico, and Border Patrol had been dealing with the fallout ever since.

As Nash locked his desk drawer, Valdez, a new agent, called out to him, "Hey, Dillon, do you have women tracking you down at work now?"

"I hope not." Nash grabbed his hat from the corner of his desk. "Someone looking for me?"

"A woman called earlier and asked if you were working today and what time you'd be off." Valdez winked. "Maybe you got a surprise waiting for you."

"God, I hope not." Nash clapped his hat onto his head. "You didn't give her any information, did you?"

Valdez's baby face sported two red spots on his cheeks. "I—I told her you were off at five."

"Valdez." Nash shook his head. "Someone needs to teach you some basics."

"Sorry. She sounded…sweet."

"They all sound sweet, Valdez—until they're not." He leveled a finger at the green agent. "Do not ever give out information like that about anyone in this office. Got it?"

"Got it, Chief." Valdez touched his fingers to his forehead. "Let me know if she *is* sweet."

Nash fired a crumpled napkin at Valdez's grinning mug and stepped into the early summer heat of the Sonoran Desert. He shook out his sunglasses and perched them on his nose before sliding into his truck.

He hoped one of those women who followed the

rodeo circuit in the Southwest hadn't tracked him down. His day hadn't put him in any mood to hang out with a woman tonight—even a sweet one.

He snorted. Not too many sweet ones around as far as he could tell.

He drove through town, grumbling under his breath about the traffic. Even Tucson drivers would scoff at his idea of traffic, but Paradiso had been growing thanks in large part to his family's groves of pecan trees. His family used to ship the pecans to be processed and packed, but some savvy business people decided to bring the processing to the pecans. The new processing plant had brought jobs, people and…traffic.

He turned onto the road that led to those pecans and his house, rolling his shoulders and blowing out a long breath. Peace, quiet and a cold beer waited for him beyond those gates.

He stopped at the front entrance to his property and picked up the mail. His tires crunched over the gravel as he made his way up the circular drive.

He threw his truck into Park and snatched his hat from the seat next to him. He exited the truck, hoisting his bag over his shoulder. He took two steps toward his porch and jerked to a halt.

A misshapen object draped with a blanket greeted him on the second step. His hand hovered over the gun in his belt.

The last delivery to a Border Patrol agent's porch had turned out to be a severed head in a box.

Nash twisted around and scanned the entrance to his driveway through narrowed eyes. Then he glanced at the camera at the corner of his house recording everything. Whoever had dropped off this present would've been captured on video.

His nerve endings alight, he stalked to the porch. Standing on the first step, he reached out and swept the powder blue blanket from the object beneath.

The *object* blinked and yawned, and Nash stared down into the face of a baby.

Chapter Two

Nash frantically scrolled through the contacts in his cell phone until he found Jaycee Lemoin. He stabbed at the name with his forefinger. The phone rang and rang on the other end without even a voice mail pickup.

"Damn it." He threw the phone at the couch and then eyed the baby, still strapped into his car seat on the floor by the door.

He'd been afraid to even pick him up. Why in the hell would Jaycee choose him as the caretaker of her baby while she went off doing God knows what?

At the kitchen table, he smoothed out the note Jaycee had left with the baby. She promised she'd be back in a day or two and just needed him to watch little Wyatt—keep him safe.

Little Wyatt gurgled from his corner, and Nash crumpled Jaycee's note in his hand and peered over his shoulder at the baby. He couldn't even turn to his friend April for help. She and his fellow agent Clay had run off to Vegas to get married and then on to Hawaii for a honeymoon. He didn't begrudge those two their happiness, but, man, he could use April right about now.

He approached the baby, who watched him coming with wide eyes. He crouched before the car seat and niggled his finger against the bottom of Wyatt's foot. He jerked back as Wyatt kicked out his legs and waved one arm.

"At least you didn't turn out to be a severed head." Nash clapped a hand over his mouth and swore. He probably shouldn't be talking to babies about severed heads...or swearing in front of them.

And that was his problem. He had no idea how to talk to babies and no idea how to care for them. He understood why Jaycee had dropped Wyatt off with him—he'd come to that girl's rescue more times than he cared to count.

Jaycee and his younger sister had been "BFFs" in high school. Who else would Jaycee turn to in Paradiso? His sister lived in New York now, and his parents had retired to Florida, leaving the care and feeding of the pecan business in his hands. But the care and feeding of a pecan was a lot easier than the care and feeding of a baby.

"You can do this, Nash. It's just a few days." He crawled to the diaper bag Jaycee had left with the baby and dragged the zipper across the top.

Another note—this one containing instructions— lay on top of an assortment of diapers, wipes, jars of baby food and bottles. Nash shook it out and read the bulleted items.

He shoved the paper into his back pocket and rubbed his hands together. "Piece of cake."

He returned to the baby and unsnapped the harness on his car seat. "Ready to get out of there, buddy?"

Wyatt reached out both arms and Nash picked him up, holding him in the air and wiggling him back and forth. "You're a good little dude. We can do this for a few days while we wait for Mom, right?"

Wyatt gurgled and some white gunk bubbled from his lips.

Still holding him at arm's length, Nash hustled into the kitchen and yanked off a length of paper towel from the roll on the counter. He wet it under the faucet and dabbed at Wyatt's chin and his little outfit with a sheep on it.

Wyatt grabbed his finger and gave him a toothless grin, moist with drool. Between the baby and the dog...

Nash spun around and lunged for the back door. He tipped back his head and called out, "Denali!"

Clay's husky appeared at the far reaches of the backyard, where the lawn tumbled into a grove of pecan trees.

"C'mon, boy. Dinnertime."

Clay and April had left him in charge of their dog when they traipsed off to get married. He'd agreed readily enough, but that was before he knew he'd have a baby under his care. Was this some kind of test? Some conspiracy to make him responsible?

Denali scampered out of the trees and raced across the backyard, skirting the pool. When he reached Nash holding Wyatt, he circled Nash's legs, wagging his tail and sniffing the baby's feet.

Wyatt's face crumpled and his bottom lip quivered.

"It's just a dog. Denali's a good boy." Nash dipped to show Wyatt the dog, and Denali lashed his tongue right across Wyatt's face.

Bad idea.

The baby wailed, and Denali barked and pranced around on his hind legs.

So much for his nice, relaxing evening. He strapped Wyatt back into his car seat and put him on the floor of the master bedroom and shut the door while he fed Denali. He'd have to keep the two of them apart. Denali had no more practice with babies than he did.

He shooed Denali back outside, where he was only too happy to roam, and then retrieved Wyatt from the bedroom.

He sat on the couch with Wyatt in his lap and pulled things out of the diaper bag, examining each item as if it were an object from an alien planet. They might as well have been.

Even for a few days, the baby needed baby stuff. Jaycee had reminded him in her note that a room in the guesthouse had been outfitted as a nursery for the last tenants his parents had before moving to Florida. He couldn't relegate Wyatt to the guesthouse, but he could drag the crib, playpen and high chair over here. He shouldn't need much more than that. Jaycee had dropped her baby off with a supply of toys and bottles and diapers.

He eyed the package of diapers he'd pulled out of the bag. Surely, that had to be enough for a little baby.

After using one of those fresh diapers on the baby, Nash secured Wyatt back in his car seat and trooped over to the guesthouse, swinging the car seat by his side. He settled the baby in the corner of the nursery and surveyed the room, hands on his hips.

He'd have to take apart the crib and reassemble it if he hoped to get it through the bedroom door. The high chair and the stroller he could wheel over and the play-pen in the living room looked collapsible.

On his way to the front of the house, he poked his head in the other bedroom and crossed to the far side of the bed with a spring in his step. A little bassinet with a canopy sat snugly beside the bed. Wyatt could sleep in this, saving him the trouble of moving the crib. That would be comfortable enough for a few days. The people who'd lived here obviously had used it for their baby.

A few hours later, all the baby accoutrements in place, Nash kicked up his feet on the coffee table and flicked Denali's ear. "We did it, boy. Wyatt's fed, changed, had a bottle, sleeping. And it's only for a few days."

THREE DAYS LATER, Nash slammed down his phone after another failed attempt to reach Jaycee.

Wyatt pounded his little fist on the tray of his high chair in solidarity and Denali barked twice.

"I'm glad we're all in agreement. Your mama is a flake." Nash leveled his finger at Wyatt and snatched it back when the baby's lip trembled. Three days and he knew that sign.

Nash had considered calling Department of Child Safety, but he didn't want to get Jaycee into trouble and Wyatt would be better off with him than in the system. He'd called in sick for two days now, and he had to start thinking about making some kind of arrangement for Wyatt's care if he hoped to get back to work anytime soon. He could check with his housekeeper, but she wouldn't be here for a few days and he didn't want to lay this on her.

He reached behind Wyatt's neck and undid the Velcro on his bib. "You ready to go for a ride, big guy?"

Denali waved his tail in the air, tickling Nash's leg with his long fur.

"Not you. There's only so much I can take of the two of you at once."

He grabbed the diaper bag with all of Wyatt's stuff in it and slung it over his shoulder. He hadn't been out with him yet. He didn't need any questions from his friends or coworkers, but he had to pick up some essentials in case Jaycee planned to take a few more days of vacation or whatever the hell she was doing right now.

He secured the base of the car seat in the back seat of his truck and snapped the carrier on top. Wyatt waved his arms and kicked his legs, which indicated excitement and happiness, and Nash eased out a sigh. He didn't need a crying baby right now.

He drove into town and pulled into the parking lot of the grocery store. He fished his crumpled list from his front pocket—formula, baby food and diapers led the necessities. He'd buy enough for the week and send Jaycee on her way with the extras.

Ducking into the back seat, he released the car seat from the base and swung it by his side as he made a bee-line for a shopping cart. He secured the car seat to the cart and wheeled it in for a shopping trip like no other.

Wyatt didn't like shopping. He fussed the entire time, and after Nash made it through checkout, he rolled the cart out the front door at breakneck speed. He got halfway to the truck before the wailing started.

He swiveled his head around to make sure nobody thought he was harming Wyatt, but no one seemed to notice the crying baby.

He stationed the cart by his truck and opened the back door to get Wyatt inside. "Hold on, buddy. Almost there."

"Do you need some help?"

At the sound of the woman's voice behind him, he jerked up, hitting his head on the door frame. "Ouch!"

"I'm sorry. I didn't mean to startle you."

Nash twisted around and his gaze met a pair of green eyes, slightly turned up at the corners, like an amused cat's.

He rubbed the side of his throbbing head. "I'll live."

Wyatt had stopped crying and squirming during the conversation, allowing Nash to snap the car seat into place. He pulled his head out of the truck, taking in the rest of the person who belonged to those eyes.

The green tank top she wore coaxed a different color from her eyes, which she blinked, as a strand of red hair floated across her cheek. He had the inappropriate urge to brush that flaming lock back from her face.

Her full lips flattened into a straight line. "You might live, but it still looks like you need help."

He gritted his teeth. He'd taken care of this baby for three days with no help from anyone. Why did this woman assume he needed help just because he was a lone man with a baby?

He patted Wyatt's chubby thigh. "He's good now."

"Maybe he is, but he's facing the wrong way."

"What?" Nash's eyebrows shot up. "Facing the wrong way?"

"He's under a year old, right?"

His heart racing, Nash flicked a glance at Wyatt and back to the woman's face. Even in his current panicked state, he noticed the sprinkling of freckles across her nose. How old was Wyatt? He didn't have a clue. He must be under one if this woman assumed he was.

"Y-yes, under one."

"Well—" she reached past him, brushing her arm against his and releasing the car seat "—he needs to be facing backward."

She unlatched the base of the car seat, twirled it around and snapped it back in place, Wyatt now pointing to the rear of the truck.

"Oh, yeah, right." Nash's cheeks warmed. Why hadn't Jaycee put that detail in her instructions? Probably because she'd intended to come back before he had a reason to take Wyatt out in the truck.

Where the hell was she?

The stranger put her finger to her lips. "I won't tell your wife you messed up."

"I don't have a wife." Nash blurted out the words

before they registered in his brain. He didn't owe this woman an explanation, but for some reason he didn't want her to think he was married.

"Oh." Her reddish gold eyebrows formed a V over her nose. "I—I just assumed… Uncle? That would explain the car seat gaffe."

Nash's jaw tightened.

"I'm so sorry." She put a hand to her chest. "I don't mean to pry. I have a thing for babies. I'm a nanny."

Chapter Three

Emily held her breath for a split second as Nash Dillon's impossibly blue eyes widened.

She continued in a rush. "I specialize in babies. So, when I saw you struggling and then noticed you had the car seat facing the wrong way, my natural instincts took over."

"A nanny?"

Nash's gaze flicked over her, head to toe, and she hoped the calf-length floral skirt, the modest tank top and the flat sandals suggested responsible nanny type.

Nash glanced at the baby in the car seat, now facing the correct way, which Emily knew about from being a cop in another life.

She wiggled her fingers at little Wyatt, and he gurgled back at her through the disgusting drool on his chin.

Nash's blue eyes lit up like someone had goosed him—not like she wouldn't want to try that. "Are you working here in Paradiso?"

Emily turned down the corners of her mouth. "I'm currently unemployed. I live in Phoenix and took a trip down to Tucson to visit a friend who's in grad school there and decided to take in Tombstone and a few other sights before heading back home and looking for a new position."

The handsome Border Patrol agent studied her face. Then he uttered the words she'd been holding out for. "I might need some help for a few days, if you don't mind working on your vacation."

"I'm always interested in helping out with babies." Had she laid it on too thick? Did people actually say things like that? Crazy people.

"I'd of course need some references, and your name would be a start."

"Of course. I wouldn't work for anyone who *didn't* do a thorough check." She pulled a newly minted business card from the side pocket of the purse strapped across her body. "Emily O'Brien."

Whenever she used a fake ID, she went with a good Irish name to match her mother's side of the family and her own red hair. Best to stay as close to the truth as possible.

She held out the card pinched between two fingers. When he reached for it, she pulled it back. "And you are?"

"I'm sorry. I'm Nash Dillon. I'm a Border Patrol agent."

She tilted her head. "You said you didn't have a wife. Is the baby yours?"

"Actually, no. I'm watching him for a friend, but I expected her back sooner and I'm afraid three days of being on my own with a baby is wearing on me."

At least he'd lasted three days. She was not sure she could do it for one day, but she had a fat paycheck waiting for her on the other end of this.

"Oh." She wrinkled her nose. "Your friend didn't abandon her baby, did she?"

"Nothing like that. She dropped him off with me. We're old friends. We go way back. Happy to help."

She extended her card again, and he plucked it from her fingers. Was he in love with Jaycee? The woman had a certain appeal, if a guy liked the soft, helpless type. Billionaire tycoon Marcus Lanier obviously did, as did Brett Fillmore, low-life druggie.

"I'm staying at the Paradiso Inn. Call me once you do your due diligence and I pass muster—if you're still interested." She tapped the card still in his hand. "My website's on there, which includes testimonials and references. Please feel free to call any one of them."

She'd been busy during her downtime when Nash had been holed up with the baby. But she knew he'd have to leave the house at some point and the tracker she'd attached to his truck told her exactly where he'd gone.

He held up the card. "Thanks, Emily. I'll be in touch."

She ducked into the truck and pinched Wyatt's foot, avoiding that whole mess on his face. "Hope to see you again, little guy. What's his name?"

"Wyatt."

She patted the baby's soft head. "Be a good boy, Wyatt."

Nash closed the door of the truck and thrust out his

hand. "Nice to meet you, Emily. I think you just might be a lifesaver."

First time anyone had called her that. She placed her hand in his, letting it rest there limply. She didn't want him to see her as any kind of aggressive threat.

"I hope I can help, Agent Dillon."

"Call me Nash."

"Well, enjoy that little bundle of joy, Nash. I look forward to hearing from you." She floated back to her rental car and slid behind the wheel, letting out a long breath. First contact successful.

She slumped in her seat and tapped her phone to call Marcus's private cell. He picked up on the first ring.

"What do you have for me?"

"Looks like I have an in. The guy Jaycee dumped the baby with needs a nanny because of course he does."

"So what? You're not a nanny. You're a fired cop who's trying to get your PI business off the ground."

Emily rolled her eyes. Nobody said you had to be brilliant to make a billion bucks. "Oh, but I *am* a nanny. I set up a fake ID and profile for myself. A quick background check on me, and he's going to believe I'm Mary freakin' Poppins."

Marcus snorted over the phone. "Don't screw it up, Emily, and where's Jaycee? Why'd she drop off Wyatt?"

"I lost her when she crossed the border. The GPS went out of range, but I thought it more important to stay with Wyatt."

"It is."

"Do you still want me to just watch Wyatt? I mean,

if I take him and bring him to you, that's kidnapping and you'll be charged."

Marcus drew a quick breath. "I never said anything about taking Wyatt. You just watch him to make sure he's okay. I'm still working with my attorneys on this end to make a move for custody."

"And when Jaycee comes back to collect him?"

"I hired you to follow Wyatt." Marcus cleared his throat. "Who's this guy who has the baby?"

"He's…" Emily squeezed her eyes closed. "Just some guy. An old friend of Jaycee's."

For some reason, she didn't want to expose Nash Dillon to Marcus Lanier's wrath or even attention. Maybe it was the light in his blue eyes or the way the sun glinted off his sandy-blond hair. Maybe it was because she wanted to protect that handsome face from some serious damage if Marcus thought Nash was standing between him and his son.

Marcus's voice roughened. "I expect a more thorough report on the guy than that when you're through with this job. I'm going to transfer another five thousand dollars into your account. I don't think being a nanny for a few days pays much."

He ended the call before she could thank him. She stashed her phone in a cup holder and took a long drink from her soda. Talking to Marcus always left a bad taste in her mouth.

As far as she knew, he'd made his money on the up-and-up, but she'd heard rumors of some shady connections. And he didn't like law enforcement. That was another reason she'd been vague about Nash's identity.

Marcus would probably blow a gasket if he found out a Border Patrol agent had possession of Wyatt.

She pulled out of the grocery store parking lot and headed back to her motel and her laptop. She had a whole lot more research to do on babies before she could convince Nash of her expertise—when in reality, she didn't even like babies.

The following day, Nash Dillon must've done his background checks because he called her cell practically at sunrise. All her fake references had come through like champions.

"It would be great if you could start today. I have to get back to work, so you and Wyatt can get to know each other."

Emily's heart skipped a few beats. Alone with a baby? How hard could that be?

"Give me your address, and I'll be over within an hour."

He obliged, even though she knew damned well where he lived—that vast house on that vast property. His family owned most of the pecan groves in the area and had a large interest in the packing plant. In other words, the Dillon family was loaded. She'd also discovered Jaycee Lemoin hailed from Paradiso and had been friends with Nash's younger sister.

She'd been thrilled to discover that last part. She'd thought maybe Nash was an old boyfriend or current lover or something. Not that it mattered to her.

When Nash ended the call, Emily darted around the room gathering her purse and a bag of tricks for the baby. She'd taken a drive up to Tucson last night to buy all the latest and greatest toys for Wyatt. She'd come in like a pro.

She drove her rental out to Nash's place, and this time she turned into the gates and circled around the driveway to park behind his truck.

She squeezed the steering wheel with her hands and huffed out a breath. "You can do this, Emily."

Pasting a smile on her face, she hitched the bag of goodies over her shoulder and strode up to the front door. Before she had a chance to ring the bell, Nash opened the door, a crying Wyatt clinging to his side.

The smile froze on her lips before she forced out some words. "Oh, what's wrong with Wyatt this morning? Is someone in a bad mood?"

"Yes." Nash scowled and then his eyes popped open. "Oh, you mean Wyatt. Yeah, I'm not sure what's going on with him."

She jumped back as a Siberian husky nosed his way between Nash's legs and barked at her.

"This is Denali. I guess he wants to get in on the action, too. You're not allergic, are you?" Nash peeled Wyatt from his shirt so that the baby hung in the air between them, his legs dangling just above the dog's head.

She should take him. That was what Nash expected. That was what any self-respecting nanny would do.

"Come here, you little rascal." She placed her hands beneath Nash's on either side of the baby, and Nash released him to her.

She pulled Wyatt against her chest, tucking one arm beneath his bottom. She couldn't very well hold him out there at arm's length.

He wrapped his hand around a strand of hair from her ponytail that had swung over her shoulder and then put it in his mouth. At least he'd stopped crying.

"Oh, no, you don't, you little—" she swallowed "—rascal." She disentangled her hair from his grubby fist.

"That's the first time he's stopped crying in about thirty minutes. You're a genius." Nash stepped aside and ushered her into the house. "He's had his breakfast. I left you instructions on what he eats when, although you're probably a better judge of that than I am."

Emily bounced Wyatt in her arms as she took a turn around what could only be described as a great room, which led into a huge kitchen completely out of her league. She noted the well-placed and discreet cameras in the corners of the room. She also recognized the type—video, no audio.

Nash may be leaving a new nanny in charge of his friend's baby, but she had no doubt he'd be keeping an eye on her.

"You have my cell phone number already, but I left it and the station number on the counter. I'm not too far, and I'll come home for lunch to check on things."

"Okay, sounds good." She dropped her bag by the couch. "What about Denali?"

"If you don't mind losing some of the AC in the house, you can leave that sliding door open so he can go in and out. He likes running around the pecan groves."

She wandered to the sliding door that led to a covered patio and a sparkling pool and those rows of trees beyond. "Maybe we'll go for a walk. Do you have a stroller?"

"I do." He jerked a thumb over his shoulder at a small hallway next to the staircase. "I put all the baby stuff in a room down here."

Emily spun around, Wyatt contentedly resting his head on her shoulder, drooling on her blouse. She tapped the list on the granite kitchen island. "I think we'll be fine."

"You are a godsend." Nash put his hands together and bowed his head. "I'll be home for lunch. Call me for anything."

He grabbed a hat, slung a laptop case over his shoulder and waved his way out the front door.

When the door slammed, Wyatt jerked up his head and his mouth puckered.

Emily pinched the list between her fingers and collapsed onto the couch with the baby, positioning him to face her on her lap. "You like Uncle Nash? I do, too, but probably for different reasons than you do."

Emily bit her bottom lip. She probably shouldn't be talking to a baby about how she had the hots for his temporary guardian.

She shook out the list and scanned it. "Food, bottle, diaper. Doesn't say anything about a nap on here. Do you want to sleep?"

As she bounced Wyatt on her knees, he brought his hands together and chuckled. The sound brought a smile to her lips. "You are pretty cute, but does that noise mean you're not interested in a nap? How about some playtime instead?"

Emily had read that babies this age liked to be on the floor to practice their rolling and crawling. She'd been relieved to discover she didn't have to carry him around all day when he wasn't sleeping.

With the baby hitched on one hip, she shooed Denali outside and shut the sliding door after him. No matter how friendly that dog seemed or how much he liked Wyatt, she'd have a lot of explaining to do if Nash came home to a baby with a dog bite.

As Denali scampered past the pool out back, Emily dug through the bag she'd brought and shook out a blanket dotted with clouds and unicorns. She spread it on the floor and placed Wyatt on his back in the middle of the square. He kicked his legs and waved his arms.

She dumped a variety of toys next to him and unfolded a padded arc that had plush cows, pigs and chickens hanging from it. She placed this over Wyatt's body, and he went nuts. He batted the primary-colored animals and gurgled with glee as they swung above him.

Leaning her back against the coffee table, she crossed her legs beneath her and watched the baby play. She'd had limited contact with the babies of a few friends back in Chicago but had never even babysat. Her father, a cop, had been too worried about her going to strangers' homes to watch their kids, so he paid her to clean the house and cook instead.

Generally, babies didn't take to her any more than she took to them, but Wyatt seemed to accept her. Maybe he just missed his mama and she was a better match for Jaycee than Nash.

Jaycee must've crossed the border after dropping

Wyatt off with Nash. Was she looking for Brett? Maybe she figured those goons who'd paid her a visit at her place in Phoenix would be tracking her and she wanted to put space between her and Wyatt so they'd believe her story.

What would those guys want with the baby, anyway? Brett must be in some big trouble. If Jaycee really feared for Wyatt's life, why not just drop him off with Marcus? They could work out the paternity and custody issues later. At least Wyatt would be safe with Marcus.

Emily's gaze tracked back to Wyatt, now gnawing on a set of giant plastic keys with his toothless gums. Maybe she should just take off with Wyatt now and bring him to Marcus. Would any judge blame him for kidnapping the baby to keep him safe from whatever threat those guys posed?

Marcus had explicitly told her not to take Wyatt. He didn't want to do anything that would prejudice a family court judge against him. And she knew more than anyone that the law followed its own protocols.

Marcus hadn't seemed too concerned when she'd reported the visit by the two men. He figured they were looking for Jaycee's boyfriend and that was the end of it. She'd tried to sound the alarm that if those two believed Wyatt was Brett's son, they'd kidnap him to use as a weapon against Brett, but Marcus hadn't seen them as a threat.

Wyatt scooted a few inches and then rocked back and forth in an attempt to roll onto his stomach. She crawled onto the blanket with him and put a toy just out of his reach to the side to encourage him.

When he finally made the big heave-ho and rolled onto his tummy, she clapped and whistled. His brown eyes got big and round when she whistled, so she puckered up and whistled a tune inches from his face. He patted her lips with his hand, and she didn't even mind the stickiness this time.

After more gymnastics on the floor, a bottle and a diaper change, which she managed by holding her breath, Emily wheeled the stroller from the room Nash had pointed out before he left.

"Let's take a walk and give that silly dog some company."

She loaded Wyatt into the stroller and found Denali's leash hanging from the front doorknob. She yelled his name in the back, and Denali emerged from the trees and scampered across the lawn. She patted her thigh. "C'mon, boy. We're going for a walk."

She hooked up the dog and pushed the stroller onto the porch. She eased it down the steps and aimed it onto the circular driveway.

The higher elevation down here made it cooler than Phoenix, although once the temperature reached over a hundred, it didn't make much difference. She crossed the road with baby and dog and steered into the grove of trees, which offered some relief from the blazing sun.

For over thirty minutes, she circled around the trees, smelling the bark and crushing the leaves in her hand. This didn't seem much like the desert.

She checked her phone for the time. "Okay, dog and baby, we need to head home for Nash's lunchtime visit to make sure we're all still alive."

A little chill snaked up her spine, and she shrugged it off as she walked into the blinding sun.

She could definitely do this for a few more days until Jaycee returned. Then wherever Jaycee went with Wyatt, she'd follow, even if it took her away from Nash Dillon.

At the edge of the trees, Emily stopped to adjust Wyatt's hat to keep the sun from his face. When a vehicle roared down the road, she squinted through her sunglasses. Wyatt hadn't given her a chance to make some lunch.

She barreled ahead with the stroller and then tripped to a stop. The engine she'd heard didn't belong to Nash's truck. A black sedan idled outside the gates of Nash's house.

Emily slowed down and stuck close to the tree line as she approached the car. Her heart slammed against her chest as she recognized the dark tinted windows and the round sticker in the back.

The thugs from Jaycee's apartment had tracked Jaycee here to Paradiso—and worse, they had a bead on Wyatt.

Chapter Four

As Nash turned onto his street, a black sedan crept up to the intersection and rolled through the stop sign to make a right. A lot of people came this way before they realized the street came to a dead end, and they couldn't drive through the pecan groves to get to the entrance to the highway. GPS steered them wrong every time, but it wouldn't kill them to stop at the stop sign on their way out.

He pulled into his driveway and dropped his stiff shoulders when he saw Emily's rental car. He knew it was a rental because he'd run the plate. Everything had checked out with Emily O'Brien, but he'd been happy he had Kyle Lewis install some security cameras in the house. He wouldn't want to have to explain to Jaycee that he'd hired a nanny from the grocery store parking lot and she'd kidnapped Wyatt.

He'd been impressed with the way Emily played with Wyatt this morning. The kid obviously knew a good nanny when he saw one. He seemed a lot more content with her than he'd been with Nash.

Had Emily come back from her walk in the time it took him to drive home?

He cut the engine, and as he stepped out of his truck, the gravel crunched behind him and he pivoted.

Emily waved from behind the stroller and dropped Denali's leash. "Hello. You're back sooner than I expected."

Denali trotted up to him, his leash dragging behind him, his tongue lolling out of his mouth in pure joy.

Nash scratched him behind the ear as he studied Wyatt, kicking his legs out in the stroller, a little hat shading his face.

Usually silence and a lonely meal greeted him when he came home from work, not this picture of domesticity. He didn't need the wife and kid, but he should get himself a dog.

He finally shifted his attention to Emily, her fiery hair in a demure braid over her shoulder. The freckles on her nose were pronounced in her pale face, and she stood behind the stroller stiffly, gripping the handle.

Nash cocked his head. "Is everything okay? Did you have a good walk?"

Her smile flashed easily across her face, too easily, and she said, "Great. Our walk was fantastic."

"I hope you're not regretting taking the job. I really need you." Nash cleared his throat. "Need your help."

Emily tossed back her braid. "Not at all. Wyatt and I had a good morning. I just wasn't expecting you back so soon. I was going to make some lunch."

"Don't bother. That wasn't in the job description." He held up the bag of food from Rosita's. "I brought lunch with me. Do you like Mexican food? Of course you do. You're from Phoenix."

"Actually, I live in Phoenix now, but I'm originally from the Midwest. I'm still getting used to some of those hot salsas." She waved her hand in front of her face as if cooling her puckered lips.

He dragged his gaze away from her mouth and pointed to Wyatt. "I guess our conversation bored him. We put him to sleep."

"Good." She ducked her head into the stroller to remove Wyatt's hat. "What I mean is, he hasn't slept all morning, not even on the walk, so he does need a nap."

Nash made a move toward the porch. "I'll let you get him to bed, and I'll set up lunch."

He held the door wide for Emily to pass through with the stroller. "We can leave that on the porch."

She shook her head so fiercely, her braid whipped back and forth. "No, I don't want to leave it out in the heat."

She skimmed past him, and his hand shot out to pluck a leaf from her hair. When she swiveled her head around, he cupped the leaf in his hand. "Looks like you took a stroll through the pecan groves."

"Are they all yours?"

He closed the door behind them and removed his hat. "They belong to my family. We used to ship them to a processing and packing plant in Texas until some partners convinced us to build one here. A lot of people in Paradiso resent that plant."

"Why should they? It must've brought jobs and a level of prosperity that a lot of these small towns down here must envy." She folded back the canopy on the stroller and slid her hands beneath Wyatt's sleeping form.

"It turned sleepy Paradiso into a real town, and a lot of the locals don't like it. Brings more of everything— more people, more traffic, more crime."

She put a finger to her lips and floated into Wyatt's makeshift nursery with Wyatt fast asleep against her chest.

Nash swung the bag of food onto the counter and got two plates from the cupboard and silverware from the drawer. He set them on the kitchen table next to the sliding doors to the back. He never used the dining room, had never used it once since moving in here after Mom and Dad took off for Florida.

He lifted the containers of food from the bag and placed them on the table.

He jumped as Emily came up behind him. He really wasn't used to having someone else in the house.

"Sorry. I didn't mean to scare you." She lifted her nose in the air and sniffed. "Smells good."

"Chicken burritos." He held up a small container of salsa. "And you can add your own heat."

"Do you like it hot?" Her cheeks sported two spots of color to rival the red of the salsa. "Spicy?"

He raised his eyebrows. So, he wasn't the only one who felt the pull between the two of them. "I do. I grew up in Paradiso, just about spitting distance to the border. Do you want some lemonade? Iced tea?"

"Some lemonade would be great." She pulled out a chair and sat down in front of one of the plates. "You mentioned crime before. Does Paradiso have a lot of crime? I wouldn't think so."

He emerged from the fridge clutching a plastic bottle of lemonade. "It's not fresh or anything."

"I grew up in the Midwest, remember? I don't think I saw a real lemon until I was a teenager." She shook out some chips onto her plate and dipped a corner into the salsa. "Crime?"

He poured the lemonade over ice in two glasses. Was she worried about her safety here in Paradiso in the home of a Border Patrol agent? "We get some crime here—mostly tweekers stealing stuff. Most of the crime happens on the border. We had a case last month…"

"What was the case?" She held her chip suspended in the air and a drop of salsa fell to the table.

"You're eating. I'll tell you later."

"My dad was a cop, homicide detective. I'm accustomed to inappropriate mealtime conversation."

He cut his burrito in half, choosing his words carefully. "We found a body without a head at the border, and then that head showed up on a fellow agent's porch. Then we found a headless body not far from the pecan groves and the second head showed up on another porch."

Emily put a hand to her heart. "Gruesome. I'm assuming those murders and decapitations were part of the drug trade."

"They were. Las Moscas."

"I've heard of them. Brutal." She crunched the chip between her teeth and dabbed the spot of salsa from the table with her napkin.

"Your father's a homicide detective? What department?"

"Retired." She waved her fork in the air. "A couple of different departments. You know what?"

"What?"

"I think my taste buds are acclimating to the cuisine because this is good." She dumped some of the salsa onto the side of her plate and dug into her burrito, running a forkful through the red puddle.

Nash shrugged and sawed off a corner of his burrito. He talked shop enough at work and with his buddy Clay. He didn't need to bring it home.

"You never told me how you came to be in charge of Wyatt. Who are his mother and father?"

Nash gulped down some lemonade. How many of Jaycee's secrets should he keep? If he told a nanny that a mother had left her baby on someone's porch, she might just get it into her head to report Jaycee to DCS. That girl had enough problems if she'd been driven to leave Wyatt with him. She didn't need a social worker on her case.

Nash ran the side of his thumb down the sweating glass. "I don't know who the father is, but the mother is an old friend, local girl, friend of my sister's."

"I suppose that means her family doesn't live here anymore."

"Long gone."

"And your sister?"

"My sister is in New York, pursuing a modeling and acting career."

Emily raised one eyebrow. "Have I seen her in anything?"

"Not unless you pay close attention to commercials."

"That's a tough life."

"She's luckier than most. She has my parents' money as a safety net." He took another bite of his food, relieved the conversation had switched from Jaycee to his sister.

"So, why did Wyatt's mom leave him here?"

Damn. Nash wiped his mouth and took another sip of his drink. "I learned a long time ago not to question Jaycee Lemoin too closely. She asked me to watch her baby for a few days, and I agreed. She's taking longer than expected, and happily I ran into you to help me out until she returns."

"Jaycee didn't let you know she'd be delayed?"

He shook his head. The peaceful domestic scene he'd encountered when he came home had turned into an interrogation. Why hadn't Emily asked him all these questions when he'd first approached her about the job?

"You know, I need to get back to work." He shoved back from the table and grabbed his plate. "Do you need anything before I leave?"

"No. Thanks for the lunch." She curled her fingers around her glass and shook it back and forth, tinkling the ice. "We never really discussed my hours. Do you want me to go back to my hotel when you get home from work, or would you like me to stick around in the evening to help out? You're paying me a generous flat fee, so I'd be more than happy to help in the evenings, too."

"That would be great." He almost suggested she move into the guesthouse, but he didn't want to freak her out. He also didn't want her asking any more questions about Jaycee. Did Jaycee really think she could just drop Wyatt off on his doorstep for a week and it wouldn't seriously impact his life?

He continued. "I'll take care of dinner, too. Any requests? Italian?"

"I can cook something."

"That's not in your job description. Taking care of Wyatt is plenty." He rinsed his plate in the sink and downed the rest of his lemonade. "Maybe he'll sleep for another hour and give you a break."

"He's a good baby." Emily rolled her eyes and blew an errant strand of hair from her face. "Compared to some of the babies I've cared for, Wyatt is an angel."

Nash mumbled under his breath, "Doesn't take after his mother."

"What?"

"Just like his mother." He waved at the door. "Thanks again, and have a good afternoon."

On his way to his truck, he tried Jaycee's number again, and again it went straight to voice mail. He didn't bother leaving a message.

That girl needed to get back to Paradiso and her baby—even if that meant Emily O'Brien would be waltzing out of his life just as smoothly as she'd waltzed into it. And he wasn't ready for that, not at all.

EMILY LIFTED THE edge of the curtain at the front window and watched Nash back his truck out of the driveway. Had the men in the black sedan stayed away because of the truck in the driveway? Would they be back?

Emily scraped the remnants of her burrito from her plate into the sink and ran the disposal. Then she sauntered to where her purse hung on the back of a kitchen chair and unhooked it. She didn't know if Nash could watch her movements from his phone or if he needed his computer to access his cameras' video feed, but she didn't want to take any chances by pulling her weapon out of her purse.

If Nash saw his nanny with a gun with the baby in the house, he'd make a fast U-turn and kick her out, maybe even call the police. But if those guys who'd paid a visit to Jaycee came back here, she wanted to be ready for them.

They must suspect that Brett was Wyatt's father. And kidnapping his son would be a surefire way of getting Brett's cooperation. They'd be disappointed and angry once they discovered Brett probably couldn't care less about his girlfriend's baby with another man. What would they do with Wyatt then?

She shivered as she plopped down on the couch and pulled her purse into her lap, the hard edge of the gun in the side pocket giving her comfort. She cupped her phone in her hand and sent Marcus a text. He hated texting, but Nash might have mics as well as cameras in the room.

She stared at the words on her phone warning Marcus that the same men who'd been around questioning Jaycee were here sniffing around Wyatt. Surely, a mother leaving her baby in dangerous circumstances would be enough to help Marcus's case for custody. Why the wait? He needed to make his move before Jaycee put Wyatt in even more danger.

As if sensing her fear, Wyatt started crying from the other room.

Emily scrambled off the couch and jogged into the makeshift nursery. Wyatt had pulled himself to his feet and stood gripping the edge of the playpen, rocking back and forth. He had opened his mouth for another howl and then blinked when he saw her and reached out his arms instead.

"I bet you need a clean diaper and a bottle. Do you like to swim? Have you been in a pool yet?"

She'd been a swimmer in high school and paid her way through college by lifeguarding and teaching swim lessons at the campus rec center. She'd taught many a toddler how to jump into the water and paddle to the edge of the pool. Wyatt wasn't exactly toddling yet, but a little pool instruction could never start too early.

Once she'd changed his diaper and given him a snack and a bottle, she tugged off his little onesie and set him on his blanket in the middle of the floor. She hadn't brought a bathing suit with her, but underwear would do in a pinch.

She tugged off her shorts and pulled her blouse over her head, all without looking at the camera. If Nash believed she had no clue about the video setup in his house, he'd trust her even more.

With her bra and panties doubling as a bikini, she scooped up Wyatt from the floor and propped him onto her hip. She hitched her purse over her shoulder and slid open the back door.

She dragged a chair poolside and dropped her purse onto it. She didn't want to be too far from her gun.

Holding Wyatt in front of her, she lowered herself to the edge of the pool and dangled her feet in the water. She put Wyatt between her legs, facing the pool, and dipped his toes in it.

He seemed to enjoy it, so Emily slid off the edge of the pool and put his bottom half in the water up to his waist. His eyes popped open wide when the water enveloped him, and then he grinned. She walked backward, pulling him along with her, and he kicked his legs like a natural.

The time spent with Wyatt passed more quickly than she'd thought possible. Clutching Wyatt to her chest, she lunged for the side of the pool and checked her phone, which she'd left in the shade of the chair. Marcus still hadn't responded to her.

She returned to the house with the baby. The sun and water had done a number on Wyatt, and after fussing for about ten minutes, he dropped off to sleep.

Emily plucked her damp underwear from her body. A few minutes in the sun would be enough to get it bone-dry. Leaving Denali on guard at the sliding door, she grabbed her purse and Nash's laptop, which he'd offered for her use, and headed back outside.

She claimed a chaise lounge on the patio, tipping an umbrella over her face but leaving her bottom half in the sun to dry off. She dragged Nash's computer into her lap on top of a towel and used the password he'd given her to log in.

She surfed the internet, watched a few videos and checked her email. Nash had some folders on his desktop, but they contained innocuous stuff like rodeo competitions and applications. She'd already done her research on him and knew he did the rodeo circuit as a hobby.

She clicked through some pictures of him in rodeo action. Damned hot. Maybe she should email a few of them to herself to drool over later when this job ended.

She launched his email, telling herself she was looking for info about Jaycee Lemoin, but he had a second log-in on his email and the computer password didn't work here.

As part of her PI prep, she'd taken quite a few online classes on computer hacking and had gotten pretty good at it. After several attempts, Nash's email program launched, displaying his inbox.

She scrolled through his messages, which mainly told her he needed to opt out of some of these mailing lists. He had a lot of junk piled up in here. He obviously kept this laptop for personal use and must have a different one for work, but occasionally he sent messages from his work laptop to this one.

These jumped out at her because of the sender's long government official email address. She had no interest in the drug trade across the border, but he'd piqued her interest with the story about the headless bodies.

She double-clicked on a couple of the work emails and scrolled through gibberish about sectors and coordinates and drone capabilities. One email had a spreadsheet attachment called Finances with a list of names.

With the mouse poised over the Close icon in the upper-right corner of the document, she scanned through them. About halfway through the alphabetical list, her gaze stumbled over a familiar name and a breath hitched in her throat.

What was Marcus Lanier's name doing in a Border Patrol agent's spreadsheet about finances?

Chapter Five

Nash put the bag of food from Mario's on the seat beside him and slammed the door of his truck. He clamped his hands on top of the steering wheel and hunched his shoulders. He should probably tell Emily about the cameras in his house.

He'd felt like a voyeur this afternoon when he'd watched her strip down to her underwear to hit the pool with Wyatt. Of course, he could've looked away.

He cranked on the engine and drove home, his mouth watering at the smell of garlic that filled the truck. First the hot salsa and now the garlic. She'd think he was trying to ward her off. Maybe he was.

He pulled in behind her car again and made a mental note to ask her about the rental. He cut the engine and gathered his stuff, the plastic bag hanging from his fingers.

When he pushed open the front door, he stuck his head into the foyer and called out, "Hello?"

Seemed strange to be doing that in his own house, but he wanted to make sure she wasn't dancing around the room in her skivvies…or less.

"We're in the kitchen eating." Emily's singsong voice drew him in with its promise of companionship and comfort. He hadn't even realized he'd been missing those things.

Denali finally tore himself away from Emily feeding Wyatt in his high chair and trotted up to him, his nails clicking on the hardwood floor.

With his hands full, Nash nudged the dog with his knee. "You're not supposed to eat garlic. I'll feed you in a minute."

"I fed him already." Emily waved Wyatt's spoon in the air. "We had quite an afternoon."

"Yeah, about that." Nash swung his laptop case on top of the opposite end of the kitchen table, where Emily was sitting next to Wyatt's high chair, and put the bag with their dinner on the counter, where a bottle of wine stood uncorked.

"I haven't been secretly drinking away the day. You mentioned Italian, so I found a bottle of red and I'm letting it breathe." She dabbed Wyatt's chin. "Hope that's okay."

"Perfect. I should've thought of that myself." He unpacked the salad and the garlic bread. "I know you aren't a lush because I have the house outfitted with cameras."

She jerked her head toward him and two red spots formed on her cheeks. "Oh. I guess you witnessed our little impromptu swim."

"Sorry. I should've told you about the cameras before."

She wrinkled her nose. "That's okay. I should've

figured you had them. I doubt you would've been so quick to leave a relative stranger in your home with your friend's baby. Besides—" she scooped up another spoonful of food from the jar "—it's not like I was skinny-dipping."

Nash swallowed and turned his attention to getting dishes for their dinner. "Wyatt must've liked the water, since you were out there for a while."

"He loved it." She touched the baby's nose. "Didn't you, my little fish?"

"You're so good with him." Nash divided the salad into two bowls and unwrapped the bread from the foil.

"Those cameras, is there audio, also? Just in case I want to break into song. I wanna warn you first."

He sucked some tomato sauce from his thumb. "No audio."

"Good." Emily stood up with the empty jar of baby food in her hand. "Wyatt had a long nap this afternoon, so I doubt he's going to be sleeping through our dinner. I'll leave him in his high chair while we eat as long as he's not fussy."

"Sounds good to me." Nash raised the bottle of wine. "You get Wyatt settled and I'll get everything ready for our dinner."

He took out a couple of place mats from the drawer next to the fridge and put them on the table. He dumped the pasta on two plates and poured the wine.

By the time he placed the silverware next to the plates, Emily was settling Wyatt back into his chair. She scattered an offering of toys on the tray and collapsed next to the high chair.

"I can take the seat of honor next to Wyatt, if you like. I mean, if you need a break." Nash tore off a corner of garlic bread and popped it into his mouth.

"I'm the nanny. I don't need a break." Picking up her wineglass, she swirled it around.

"Even nannies need breaks." He grabbed his own glass and touched it to hers. "Here's to fortuitous meetings in grocery store parking lots and fate."

"Yeah...fate." She clinked his glass and took a gulp of wine.

Nannies didn't need breaks? She guzzled that cab as if her sanity depended on it.

"Whoa, that's good." She placed the glass on the table and stabbed at her salad with a fork. "What does your job entail?"

Nash blinked. "My job?"

"Border Patrol agent. What do you do mostly? Is it people, drugs, both?"

"There are different sectors down here that report to Tucson, and we deal mostly with drug interdiction in Paradiso. That's our main focus. We don't have many illegal border crossings on our end."

"Is there one cartel in particular in this area?"

"We encounter them all, but Las Moscas is the main source of drug smuggling along the border here."

"The decapitated people?"

He nodded. "Las Moscas."

"The cartels have...collaborators on this side of the border? People who finance them? People who move their product?"

"You *are* your father's daughter, aren't you?"

The glass in her hand jerked, and a few droplets of wine stained the tablecloth. "Why do you say that?"

"I don't know. Most women aren't interested in my job." He pushed back from the table and yanked the dish towel from the oven door and ran it under the faucet.

He returned to the table and dabbed at the red spots on the white material.

"I'm sorry. Let me." She made a grab for the dish towel, but he held firm.

"I've got it." He waved the towel at Wyatt. "Besides, I think your charge needs another toy. He's thrown all of his on the floor."

Emily leaned over. "Wyatt, Denali has slobbered over all your toys. Do you think it's okay to give Wyatt a piece of this bread to suck on?"

Nash lifted his shoulders. "You're the nanny. Will he choke?"

"I—I was just wondering how garlicky it was. He might not even like it." She pulled the soft center from a piece of bread and put it to Wyatt's lips.

The baby sucked the bread into his mouth and then spit it out onto his tray.

"I guess there's your answer—no garlic for dogs or babies." He picked up the bottle of wine. "Do you want a refill?"

Pinging her fingernail against the half-empty glass, she shook her head. "I still have to drive back to my motel, and one glass is my limit for driving."

"Very responsible of you, but then I suppose a cop's daughter would be careful." He splashed another few sips of wine into his own glass. "I'm not driving, so I'll live dangerously and have another half a glass. I somehow don't think babysitting and alcohol mix, do you?"

"Definitely not. I once witnessed a mother smoking weed right in the presence of her baby." Emily reached out and stroked her knuckle across Wyatt's cheek. "A baby about the same age as Wyatt. Don't you think someone like that is an unfit mother?"

"Me?" Nash inclined his head. "I thought you were the expert. Yeah, I suppose anything that alters your capacity to react quickly would interfere with taking care of a kid."

"The courts usually award custody to mothers, but sometimes fathers make a better guardian."

Her words had a lilt at the end, as if she were confirming her beliefs with him. Being a bachelor with not much contact with kids, he'd never given these issues much thought. Once Jaycee came back to get her son, he wouldn't think about them again.

He lifted his shoulders. "I suppose when drugs and alcohol are involved, that changes the situation. Do you want any more to eat? We have leftovers."

"I'm good." She pushed away her plate of half-eaten pasta. "I'll wrap this up and have it for lunch tomorrow…if I'm still coming."

"I haven't heard from Wyatt's mother yet, so I hope so."

"You can't call her?"

"She doesn't answer, or her phone is turned off."

"You'd think she'd want to hear how Wyatt's doing."

"She trusts me." *If only he could trust Jaycee.*

Emily jumped up from the table. "I'll help you clear the dinner dishes and get Wyatt comfy. He'll need another bottle before he goes to bed. Maybe that'll make him sleepy."

"I hope so. He's been waking up in the middle of the night, and it takes me a while to get him back to sleep." Nash stood up next to Emily and took the plate from her hand. "You go do nanny business and I'll take care of the kitchen."

She plucked Wyatt from his high chair and carried him off to the other room.

Nash put away the leftovers and rinsed the dishes to stack in the dishwasher. He'd feel a lot better if Emily and Wyatt moved into the guesthouse, but he felt selfish for asking. She'd been with the baby all day. Of course, he could offer her more money to stay the night.

If Jaycee spent another full day away, he'd propose the plan to Emily. She was getting suspicious about Jaycee, and he didn't blame her. What kind of mother dropped her baby off with a friend and disappeared, refusing to answer her phone?

And he hadn't even told Emily *how* Jaycee dropped off Wyatt—on his porch like a foundling. Emily would be horrified and might even threaten to call DCS. She'd already been attacking the court system that seemed to favor mothers over fathers, regardless of the circumstances.

Her vehemence surprised him. Had her father the cop told her stories? She didn't seem eager to talk about him, even though she clearly had an interest in law enforcement. Maybe they'd had a falling-out. He knew enough cops to know they could be hell to get along with on the home front.

Border Patrol agents were no picnic, either.

Every woman he'd ever dated had seemed more interested in his family's business than his own. It had made him suspicious, standoffish. His friend April called him superficial.

As Nash swept up the last of the crumbs from the kitchen table, Emily returned, bouncing Wyatt in her arms.

"He's a little frisky, so he might need some playtime before his bottle and bed." She pointed to a blanket folded on top of the coffee table. "I don't know if you saw on your super-duper camera, but I had him out on the blanket on the floor with some toys around him. He practices rolling and getting up on his hands and knees. He can't actually crawl yet, but he rocks back and forth, which is a precursor to crawling."

"We'll give it a try, right, buddy?" Nash poked Wyatt in his belly, which got a laugh out of him.

"I hope his mother doesn't miss any of his firsts in her absence." Emily sucked in her bottom lip. "You'd think she wouldn't want to miss a thing."

"If he starts crawling, I'll capture it on my phone." Nash patted the pocket of his shorts.

Emily seemed determined to attack Jaycee—not that she didn't deserve it.

"I'll leave my toy bag here for tomorrow, and I'll even bring a swimsuit." She winked as she turned Wyatt over to him.

He and Wyatt stood at the front door and waved Emily into her car.

Setting Wyatt in the middle of the blanket on the floor worked wonders. The little guy got up to all kinds of new tricks on his own, so Nash reached for his laptop and pulled it onto his thighs as he stretched his legs out next to Wyatt's play area.

He entered his password and launched the web browser. He hovered the mouse over the history tab and then said, "Hell, you saw her in her bra and panties. Snooping into her internet searches is nothing."

And it was nothing. She'd watched some music videos and a short documentary on Mount Everest. She'd even checked out a few baby sites. Must want to keep up on all the latest trends in childrearing.

He closed out of her browsing history. The woman deserved a little privacy. Had he been expecting her to read how-to articles on kidnapping or something?

He launched his email. He squinted at the new messages loading and then leaned back against the couch and crossed his arms. The new emails scrolled in from about three o'clock this afternoon even though he hadn't launched his email program since last night.

He sat up. Emily had gotten into his email.

EMILY SWUNG BY a liquor store on her way back to the motel. She pulled into a space in front of the plate glass window and threw the car into Park. She slumped down in the seat, gripping her phone.

Marcus still hadn't responded to her message about the thugs sniffing around Wyatt. She eked out a little sigh of relief. She didn't know what to say to Marcus right now.

Why did a Border Patrol agent have Marcus's name in connection to the cartels? Of course, finances could mean anything. She'd done her research on Marcus Lanier before taking the job, and it hadn't been difficult. Everyone in Phoenix knew about Marcus.

He had his fingers in many pies around the city, and he seemed to have the Midas touch. He made money and he made other people money. And he spent money.

Whatever passed for a social scene in Phoenix, Marcus Lanier took center stage in that scene—he and his perfect wife. Did that perfect wife know he fooled around on the side? Probably. Did she know he'd fathered a baby with his side piece, Jaycee Lemoin? Probably.

If Marcus had hired her to keep tabs on Wyatt and gather evidence against Jaycee to take her to court for custody, Ming Lanier would have to know about her husband's infraction.

But the public didn't necessarily know what the Border Patrol knew. Were all of Marcus's enterprising ventures covers for his real business, drugs?

"Damn." Emily shoved her phone into the side pocket of her purse and flung open the car door. She may be using dirty money.

She stalked into the liquor store and made a beeline for the wine section. Might as well stay with the same poison. After the day she'd had, she needed more than that half glass of wine with dinner. But Nash had been right. Her father had drilled into her the evils of drinking and driving.

She grabbed a bottle of merlot by the neck and charged up to the register. Dad never said anything about drinking and watching TV, though.

She paid for the wine and slid back into her car. She drove to her motel and parked as close to her room as she could get. Paradiso had a limited number of lodging choices, but it was hardly a hot spot for tourism. Bisbee and, of course, Tombstone drew the lion's share of visitors to this area. Paradiso wasn't even near a well-traveled border crossing—at least not a legal one. She'd read that the border here was porous with tunnels used for the trafficking of drugs and even people.

She dug her key card from her purse and then hung her bag over her shoulder. She grabbed the wine and exited her vehicle.

The streets of Paradiso rolled up early. Most of the restaurants and bars still open lined the main drag through town, and this little gem of a motel was definitely off the beaten track.

Pinching her key card between her fingers, she walked toward her room. As she passed the stairs that led to the second floor, a shadow moved across the wall.

Instinctively, she reached for the side pocket of her purse where her gun nestled, but it was too late.

An arm shot out and ripped the purse from her shoulder. She started to wield the bottle of wine like a club. Her attacker grabbed it and dropped it to the patch of grass under the stairs. Then he dragged her toward an open door she hadn't noticed before now and shoved her into a utility room.

A low voice growled in her ear, "Make one noise, and you're dead."

In case she hadn't gotten the message, her assailant jabbed the barrel of a gun beneath her ribs.

Chapter Six

Emily gulped in breaths of air as the man held her from behind, curling one arm around her neck.

"Who is that baby to you?"

"What baby?"

He tightened his hold and she choked. "The baby at the Border Patrol agent's house. Who is the baby to you and who is he to that cop?"

Should she tell him? Should she just blurt out the truth that Marcus Lanier was the baby's father? Wouldn't they leave Wyatt alone once they knew Brett wasn't the father?

She gulped. She had no authority to reveal that information. That was the one thing she'd promised Marcus—she'd never tell a soul Wyatt was his child, not until he was ready to do so. Even to save Wyatt's life?

Marcus should've taken her warnings seriously about the men who'd threatened Jaycee. Did he not believe her?

For now, Wyatt was safe with Nash. That was why this guy had gone after her. They knew Nash Dillon was Border Patrol and they knew better than to mess with the law. That bought her a little time.

He drilled the gun into her side. "Answer me. What do you know?"

She clawed at his arm and he relented a fraction of an inch. She coughed.

"I don't know anything about the baby. The Border Patrol agent is my friend and the baby belongs to his friend who had an emergency. I don't know the mother. I don't know anything."

He released her, giving her a push forward. That didn't fool her for a minute, as she still felt the weapon up close and personal. She eyed her purse on the ground outside the utility room.

The man didn't know she had a gun in there, but she didn't plan to use it unless her life was in imminent jeopardy. If she dove for her purse, yanked out her .22 and shot him between the eyes, she'd have a lot of explaining to do—to everyone.

"I'll tell you what, *pelirroja*. You're gonna help us."

"Me?" Her voice squeaked as much from surprise as the pressure that had recently been applied to her windpipe. That was not what she'd expected from him.

"How am I going to help you? I told you. I don't know anything. If you're the baby's father, I suggest you go through the proper channels to—"

"Shut up." He slugged her in the back and her knees buckled.

"Are you going back there tomorrow?"

"No. I'm leaving Paradiso tomorrow." She gritted

her teeth against the throbbing pain right above her kidney.

"You lie, *pelirroja*." His hot breath stirred the hair at the back of her neck, and she shivered. "You're gonna go back there tomorrow, and when the cop goes back to work after lunch, you're gonna take the kid for a walk—away from the cameras at his house. Then you're gonna turn that kid over to us. You got it?"

She nodded. What else could she do at this point? If she refused, he'd inflict more pain on her. She had a feeling he liked administering pain.

"Wh-why do you want him? Are you going to hurt him?"

He shoved her away from him and she stumbled against the wall. "Don't worry about it. And if you get any bright ideas? We will kill that kid. Kill you. Kill the cop. And even kill that mutt. Got it?"

"Yes."

"Stay there against the wall until you hear a car drive by. And if you call the police? Let's just say that goes under the category of bright idea and it'll have the same ending. It might take longer, but we always get our man...and baby, if it comes to it."

Her muscles rigid, Emily froze in place until she heard the sound of an engine roll by. She spun around and flew out of the utility room. Dropping to her knees, she scrabbled for her purse on the ground and pulled out her gun.

She had nobody to shoot, but she wasn't going to go to her room without this baby in her hand. She grabbed the bottle on the grass and pressed it to her chest. Thank goodness it hadn't broken. She needed that wine more than ever right now.

With her knees trembling, she wobbled to her room and slipped inside. She threw the chain and slid to the floor, the bed at her back, pointing her gun at the door.

After several minutes and several deep breaths, she staggered to her feet and placed her weapon on the credenza. She screwed open the bottle and poured the wine all the way to the top of a plastic cup.

She gulped half of it before she sank down at the foot of the bed. Maybe she should kidnap Wyatt tomorrow morning and drive back to Phoenix with him and deposit him with Marcus. She could make a good case to a judge why she felt it was in the baby's best interest to leave Paradiso and bring him to his biological father. No family court judge in their right mind would blame Marcus for doing that after what she'd just been through.

She bounded up from the bed and fished her phone from her purse. Still no message from Marcus. Did he think she was joking? Overreacting? He wouldn't think that once she told him what happened tonight.

She didn't have a plan yet, but she sure as hell wasn't turning Wyatt over to those maniacs.

IN THE MORNING, Nash adjusted the angle of the camera in the corner of the living room, but if Emily took his laptop out to the patio again, he wouldn't catch her in the act of snooping through his email. He couldn't take the laptop with him today. She'd be suspicious. Maybe that would be a good thing, a subtle hint that he knew she'd been into his email.

How'd she get into it, anyway? He'd password protected it. It probably wouldn't take a tech genius to bypass an email password, but Emily was a nanny. Wasn't she?

All her references checked out and she even had an online presence, but if passwords could be hacked, identities could be forged.

Nash ran a hand through his hair. She could just be a nosy nanny.

He grabbed the laptop and stuffed it into his bag. She could think what she wanted. He didn't have any top secret info on his computer, but he didn't like the idea of someone spying on him.

Wyatt crowed from his high chair, and Nash ran a thumb across the baby's soft hair. "I know you like her, buddy, and so do I, but I've had enough duplicitous women in my life to last me—starting with your mama."

The doorbell made him jump, even though he'd been expecting Emily any minute.

Denali got to the door first and barked.

"I know." Nash patted the husky's head. "You like her, too."

He swung open the door, and Emily lifted her hand in a wave. "Reporting for duty, unless Wyatt's mom decided to return and whisk him away."

"Not back yet. I'm sure I'll hear something today." He widened the door and stepped to the side.

As she crossed the threshold, Denali jumped, landing his paws against her side. Emily winced and staggered backward.

"Whoa, boy." Nash placed a hand on Emily's back to steady her. "Are you okay?"

"He just took me by surprise." She grabbed Denali's head and touched her nose to his wet, black one. "How are you, Denali?"

"I fed him already, and I gave Wyatt a bottle and put him in his high chair. I didn't feed him any food, though." He grabbed his bag and hat. He wanted to get out of here so she wouldn't notice the missing laptop.

She dropped a backpack on the kitchen table and leaned in to give Wyatt a kiss on his head. "Hello, big guy. Missed you."

Nash cocked his head as he watched Emily stroke Wyatt's hair. Her voice sounded almost shaky. She really did care about him. "I have to run, Emily. Do you have everything you need? I'll stop by for lunch again."

"We're fine." She jabbed her finger at the backpack. "I even brought a swimsuit today. Wyatt liked the water so much, I'll make a swimmer out of him."

But you won't be surfing the internet and my email after the swim this time.

Nash cleared his throat. "You two have a great morning. If there's anything you need…anything you want to ask me, you have my number."

Emily's head jerked up, her green eyes wide. "L-like what?"

"Like… I don't know. Whatever." He chucked Wyatt under the chin and then strode to the front door with Emily right on his heels.

She stood at the door with her purse still strapped across her body, her hand resting on the outside flap as if ready to leave.

When he got to his truck, he turned and waved.

Emily nodded, but she seemed to be looking over his head at the driveway that wound down to the street.

Knots formed in his gut as he drove away from the house. Emily's smiles and good cheer had seemed forced this morning. Her jumpiness made him second-guess everything. He'd be keeping a close eye on the video feed this morning.

At the office, Nash got ready for an online meeting with a forensic accountant. They were digging into the finances of Las Moscas. They knew there had to be some major money-laundering schemes on this side of the border, and they were investigating several suspects.

Nash brought up the spreadsheet that contained the list and several notes he'd already made on each. While he waited for the meeting to start, he set up his personal laptop next to his work computer. Had Emily noticed it missing yet?

With several taps of the keyboard, he brought up his security system and watched Emily cleaning up Wyatt after breakfast. The kid seemed thrilled with her. That was all that mattered right now. So, she was a snoop. Maybe she wanted to find out more about him. Or was that just wishful thinking on his part?

The two meals they'd shared yesterday felt like dates—except for the presence of Wyatt at dinner. He liked her, liked talking to her, and their attraction was undeniable. Again, wishful thinking?

"Good morning, Agent Dillon. Sorry I'm late."

Nash shifted his attention from his personal computer to his work computer and the face of Special Agent Webb filling his screen. "Good morning, Agent Webb. Right on time."

"My name's Bruce. Can I call you Nash?"

"Absolutely." Nash took a sip of coffee. "I have my list up and can take notes as we talk. Who do you want to discuss first?"

"Probably the guy I got the most hits on. His name is Marcus Lanier. He's a Phoenix businessman, a real mover and shaker. He's married to Ming Lee Hong, daughter of a wealthy entrepreneur in China. We're not sure his father-in-law is on the up-and-up, either."

"Makes sense. The wife went from one criminal family to another. What do you have on the guy?"

While Webb went on about anomalies in Lanier's finances, Nash multitasked. He listened to Webb, made notes in his spreadsheet and kept one eye on Emily and Wyatt.

After about an hour discussing two of the possible Las Moscas contacts, Webb started to wrap up. "I'm going to send you Lanier's and Booker's latest payments and withdrawals for your files. It's not like you're gonna find any payments to drug dealers in there, but they serve to outline and support some of what I've been talking about this morning. We can set up another meeting to discuss a few of our other suspects, but I wanted to get to those two first. I have the file, and you'll have the file. That's it. We're not spreading this info around just yet."

"Sounds good, Webb. You guys are thorough."

"I love numbers, man. What can I say?" Webb chuckled and signed off.

Nash waited a few minutes for Webb's email to come through with the attachment. He clicked on it and saved the file to his computer.

Then he stood up and stretched. Taking another glance at his security feed, Nash turned with his coffee cup in hand to get a refill.

Valdez beat him to it, filling up his commuter mug.

"Leave some for the rest of us. What are you fueling up for?"

Valdez's lips twisted. "You missed it while you were in your meeting, but it looks like we have a body at the border."

"Damn. You going out?"

"Yeah, I'm lead on this one." Valdez swallowed. "It's almost in the next sector, so we'll probably be out all afternoon."

"Decapitation?" Nash grabbed the coffeepot from Valdez's none-too-steady hand.

"Not sure yet. Drone picked it up and I was the lucky one monitoring the drone footage, so it's mine."

"You'll do fine, Valdez." Nash gave the green agent some tips before he set off for the border, and then returned to his much less exciting work on finances.

He had done most of the work on the map of tunnels they'd received from April Archer. Nash had the backbreaking job of investigating most of those tunnels, so it was his turn to sit in the office now and look at numbers. With Wyatt's arrival, it couldn't have happened at a better time.

How did Jaycee know he wouldn't be on the border for days and unable to care for Wyatt? Jaycee didn't think. He'd been happy when his sister, Eve, had gotten the harebrained notion to run off to New York to study acting, just because it had separated her from Jaycee. She'd had their parents' money behind her to explore this whim. Jaycee didn't have a dime. Did she have a husband?

Nash blew out a breath as he sat behind his desk, setting down his coffee cup next to his computer. A quick glance at his laptop showed him all was well with Emily and Wyatt.

He grinned as he watched Wyatt's antics on the floor. Emily was right—if Jaycee didn't return soon, she would miss her son's first attempts at crawling.

Nash cracked his knuckles and opened his folder on Aaron Booker. He dragged the newest financial info from Webb into the folder and then opened it. He scanned through the expenses. This guy definitely lived the high-life, but he had the income to support it—at least on the surface. Webb would dig into the money source and get to the bottom of the pit.

Nash also had a folder on Lanier and repeated the actions he'd performed for Booker. Lanier lived a similar lifestyle. Nash's eye scanned down the expenses and the payees when he stumbled across a familiar name.

Lanier had transferred five thousand dollars into the

account of an Emily Lang. But his nanny's last name was O'Brien. Emily wasn't an unusual name.

He shook his head and moved on, but Emily Lang's name popped up again—another five-thousand-dollar transfer. Lanier had made no notes with the transfer. It could be anything, but why the same amount and why two…no, three payments to this Emily Lang?

Webb had delved deeper than a cursory look at finances ever could. Nobody would be able to track these transfers, not the IRS, not Lanier's wife.

Maybe Emily Lang was a high-priced escort.

Nash closed the file and turned to other work, but a persistent feeling of unease had him by the back of the neck.

Why had Emily been looking through his private emails? Why had she turned up in the grocery store parking lot at precisely the moment he needed her? Why would a woman on vacation be willing to work for a few days for a stranger?

Nash dragged his work computer keyboard toward him. With his fingertips buzzing, he launched a search engine and entered *Emily Lang*.

Emilys from around the country popped up—Realtors, city council members. He couldn't go through them all.

He went back to the top of the page and entered *Emily Lang Chicago*. That didn't help. The same amount of Emilys filled his screen.

With his heart thudding, Nash switched gears and accessed the National Crime Information Center database. He wiped his brow with the back of his hand and entered *Emily Lang*.

He held his breath as several Emily Langs populated the display. He looked into each one, but none of them matched the pretty redhead currently at his house.

Okay, she wasn't a felon. That was because she wasn't Emily Lang.

Nash swirled his coffee in the mug and stared into the brown whirlpool. He placed it carefully on the blotter and wiped his hands together. Then he entered *Homicide Detective Lang*.

Several articles popped up and Nash opened the first one. He read aloud, "'Chicago homicide detective Joseph Lang was shot and killed while chasing a suspect in the East Side Strangler investigation.'"

He perused a few more articles on the murder of Detective Lang. The SOB who'd killed him had been shot later in another shoot-out. Good riddance.

Nash clicked to the next page of search results and hovered over another article. Apparently, Lang's daughter had gone into police work, too, and had gotten herself fired. Nash clicked on the article, and his mouth dropped open.

The red hair was shorter and the green eyes sadder, but he'd found Emily Lang, and the disgraced police officer was in his house under false pretenses…alone with Jaycee's baby.

Chapter Seven

Were they watching the house? Emily peeked out the front curtains for the hundredth time that morning. The man last night had seemed so sure she'd be meeting him with Wyatt in hand after lunch. What would they do if she didn't show?

They didn't want to come to Nash's house. If they did, they would've made an attempt already. They wanted to stay off Nash's radar.

If they weren't watching the house, how would they know if she left early this morning with Wyatt? They must be tracking her. If she didn't make the meeting, they'd know where and how to find her.

How had they tracked her to the motel last night? She knew she hadn't been followed from Nash's place to the liquor store. They must be keeping tabs on her the same way they'd followed Jaycee down here and the same way she'd followed Jaycee down here—GPS device on her car.

She'd have to get it off and then make her move. She'd leave a note for Nash so he wouldn't think she was a straight-up kidnapper. She'd keep it vague enough and then contact him when she got Wyatt safely into Marcus's hands.

Not that Nash would believe her or let the abduction of Wyatt stand. He'd come after her for sure. He'd put an APB on her car, which she would ditch. He'd call in the police.

She'd have to evade law enforcement, the thug from last night and Nash Dillon—all with a baby in tow. Hell, she'd been a cop herself for all of three years. She could handle them all.

With Nash keeping an eye on her via those cameras, she'd have to make her movements look natural. She should've told Nash that she'd planned to take Wyatt to the park today. Leaving with him in his car seat would be the most natural thing ever.

She could always disable those cameras, but he'd probably freak out. He'd taken his personal laptop to work with him today. Either he knew she'd been looking through his stuff or he didn't quite trust her.

She patted Wyatt's back as he slept in the bassinet that she'd had Nash take down from his room upstairs. She'd been gradually loading up Wyatt's toys in her bag throughout the morning.

With her purse over her shoulder and her hand hovering near the weapon zipped inside, she slipped through the front door and sauntered to her car. She ducked down on the side of the car away from the cameras stationed at the front of the house. On her knees, she swept her phone across the undercarriage of the rental.

She got a hit. She reached beneath the car and felt

along the wheel well, her fingers dancing along the greasy surface. They stumbled over a round disc, and she peeled it off the car.

She couldn't throw it away or even move it and give away the fact that she'd found the device. She dropped it on the ground and shoved it to the center of the car so she wouldn't roll over it and crush it on her way out.

They had to think she was still here waiting for the afternoon appointment.

Squatting on the gravel driveway, she brushed her fingers together and popped up. She hustled back into the house and opened the sliding door to the back, emitting a high-pitched whistle. "Denali!"

She heard the dog bark in the distance and hung on the door, waiting for him. When he ran up to her, she scratched his head. "You're a good boy. I wish we could take you with us for protection, but I can't kidnap a baby *and* a dog and leave Nash with…nothing."

A little sob bubbled up her throat. Nash would think poorly of her only until she could fully explain. Then he'd understand why she had to get Wyatt away from here.

Denali stood at attention at the foot of the bassinet. If she'd been anyone else trying to remove Wyatt from this house, Denali would've raised a fuss. But he trusted her…just like Nash trusted her.

She bent over the bassinet and scooped up Wyatt. "Do you want to meet your daddy? He may not be ready, but it has to be now."

Marcus still hadn't answered her texts, but he might be avoiding communication with her. Maybe his wife had gotten ahold of his burner phone and he was in damage mode.

She still didn't understand why he was in a Border Patrol spreadsheet, but maybe she'd misunderstood. Maybe those people were donors or fund-raisers or something. She knew Marcus had connections with law enforcement in Phoenix and often contributed to their causes.

With Denali standing guard over Wyatt, she grabbed a piece of junk mail from Nash's counter and scribbled him a note full of apologies and a few explanations. She wanted him to know that she had Wyatt's best interests at heart and was taking him to his father. She placed the note in the center of the counter, held in place with the half-full wine bottle from last night. He couldn't miss it.

She settled a sleepy Wyatt in his car seat and strapped him in. Nash hadn't said she couldn't take Wyatt in the car, so hopefully he wouldn't see anything unusual in her actions. He might not even be watching her right now. He had a job to do. He couldn't stay glued to his security feed all day.

She hitched her bag of goodies over her shoulder and hoisted up the car seat. She smacked a kiss in the air. "Bye, Denali. Be a good boy."

She locked the front door and trudged to her car, Wyatt swinging next to her. Nash had transferred the car seat base from his truck to her car for just this reason—well, not this *exact* reason, but he shouldn't be alarmed that she was taking Wyatt for a drive.

She snapped his car seat into the base in the back

seat—facing backward. That had been her in with Nash in that grocery store parking lot. Of course, if it hadn't been advice about the car seat, she would've come up with something else. Nash had been so primed for help, and she'd pounced on his weakness.

She got behind the wheel and swiped a sniffle from her nose as she pulled away from Nash's house, leaving the GPS tracker in the driveway. By the time one o'clock rolled around, she'd be in Phoenix.

Marcus should be able to protect Wyatt when she got to his place and even admit to being the baby's father. Her attacker and his sidekick would have no use for Wyatt at that point. They could get their man another way.

She'd had a feeling even if she'd told the guy last night that Wyatt wasn't Brett's son, he wouldn't have believed her. Or maybe he wouldn't have cared. They'd figured out that Jaycee was lying about Wyatt, so they knew he was *her* son, and if Brett cared anything about Jaycee and her baby, he might be willing to make a deal.

She rolled up to the end of Nash's road and turned right, away from the town. She could take a back road to the freeway and wouldn't have to pass through Paradiso and the Border Patrol office on her way out.

This was going to work.

Emily accelerated, but not too much. She didn't need to get pulled over for a ticket or draw attention to herself in any way. She checked her rearview mirror and her heart did a flip.

A truck, traveling at a high speed, a cloud of dust

in its wake, had appeared behind her out of nowhere. Had they been watching and waiting for her instead of depending on the GPS tracker? They had no way of knowing she'd find that device. They didn't know her profession…or former profession.

She applied more pressure to the gas pedal, but she didn't plan to get into a high-speed chase with Wyatt in the back seat of her car. Lodging her tongue in the corner of her mouth, she glanced in her mirror again.

The truck was gaining on her, and then she blinked and adjusted the mirror as if that could change what she saw.

That white truck looked an awful lot like Nash's truck. She couldn't afford to see him right now, either. She could tell him she was taking Wyatt for a drive to calm him down, but then how would she escape?

What was he doing home this early, anyway? He'd told her he would be coming home at lunchtime, and he sure as hell didn't see her leaving on the cameras and drive this far this fast from his office.

Maybe that wasn't even Nash. Lots of people drove white trucks in this town. She squinted in her rearview and swore. No mistaking the aviator sunglasses. That was Nash on her tail.

She'd have to pull over, or he'd know for sure she was absconding with Wyatt. She eased off the pedal and put on her signal. Gripping the steering wheel with sweaty palms, she veered toward the side of the road and shifted into Park without turning off the engine. Not that she could make a quick getaway with Nash standing beside her car.

As he pulled in behind her, she wiped her hands on her skirt and pasted a smile on her face. "You sure you don't want to start crying back there to bolster my story, Wyatt?"

The baby gurgled and burped up some white gunk, clearly not appreciating the seriousness of the situation, although the gunk on his onesie might indicate an upset baby.

She winked at him in the mirror. "Good boy."

Emily buzzed down her window as Nash drew near, his hand hovering over the weapon on his hip. Force of habit? Did Border Patrol agents make traffic stops?

She called out in a singsong voice, "Hey, you. What are you doing home so early?"

"Cut the engine." His tone lashed her, and she jerked her head back from the window.

She also obeyed his command, her fingers fumbling with the keys in the ignition. She left them swinging there. He must be angry that she'd taken Wyatt for a ride without telling him first.

She ran her tongue along her dry teeth. "Wyatt was cranky and restless, so I thought a drive might calm him down."

"Stop with the lies, Emily, and get out of the car. Put your hands where I can see them. You know the drill, Officer Lang."

Her blood ran cold in her veins. Busted. How had he discovered her true identity?

"I—I can explain. I don't mean any harm to Wyatt."

"Stick your hands through the open window and

step out, keeping them in front of you, when I open the door."

She swallowed and slid a glance to the side. At least he didn't have his weapon drawn, but that could change if she didn't comply.

She twisted to her left and stuck her hands out the window, wiggling her fingers to show him she didn't have anything.

He stepped toward the door, the leather of his equipment belt creaking. She knew the sound of that belt intimidated suspects—and she understood why.

The doors of her car had automatically unlocked when she turned off the engine, and Nash reached over and opened the door with her arms hanging through the window.

She *did* know the drill—had applied it many times herself before she went rogue. She stepped out of the car with her arms still outstretched, and she looked at her reflection in his sunglasses for a split second before he commanded her to turn around and face the car.

She pulled her arms from the open window and turned toward the car, looking at Wyatt in the back seat kicking his legs in excitement at the sound of Nash's voice.

"Hands on the car, legs apart. Do you have any weapons on you?"

"C'mon, Nash. I'm not kidnapping Wyatt." Well, technically she *was* kidnapping Wyatt, but it was for a greater good. She'd make Nash see that once he stopped this tough-cop routine.

He nudged her leg to the side with his boot and patted her down—not exactly how she'd imagined their first physical contact to go.

"Any weapons in the car?" His voice dismissed any familiarity or…fondness between them.

"In the side pocket of my purse on the passenger seat—a .22 Smith & Wesson."

He sucked in a breath behind her and slammed the driver's-side door shut. "Now you're gonna tell me what the hell you want with Jaycee Lemoin's baby. Then I'm gonna call the police to pick you up for attempted kidnapping."

"Like this?" She lifted one hand from the car. "Can we talk like reasonable people?"

"Are you a reasonable person, Emily? Do reasonable people lie about who they are to get close to…a baby and then take off with that baby? Do reasonable people create identities and references and fake lives?"

"Private investigators do when they're working a case."

"A case? Wyatt is a case?"

"Yes, he is. I'm working for his father. I'm trying to keep him safe because he is in danger, and not just from his flighty mother, whom you seem to have a soft spot for to the extent of protecting her when she doesn't deserve it. Jaycee abandoned her baby, and you know it."

A car sped by in the other direction and honked. Emily jumped. The longer she stood exposed out here with Wyatt in the car, the better the chance the real criminals would move in on them.

"You're working for Wyatt's father?" He prodded her in the back with his knuckle. "Turn around."

With her hands out to her sides, she rolled on the car to face him. "Wyatt's father hired me to keep an eye on Wyatt until he can get his results back from a DNA test and make a move for custody."

"You can drop your hands."

Nash pushed his sunglasses on top of his head, and Emily let out a breath when she finally got to look into those blue eyes. She could make him understand better when he was the Nash she knew instead of the law.

"Is that his story, or are you lying to me…again?"

"Story? It's not anybody's story. A client hired me in Phoenix to follow Jaycee and the baby. When Jaycee split off from the baby, my orders were to stay with Wyatt, which I did."

"Stay with Wyatt until you could kidnap him? What kind of father would do that to the mother of his child?"

"No." She shook her head, and a gust of wind from a passing car whipped her hair across her face. She pushed it out of the way and held it in a ponytail. "The kidnapping was my idea."

Nash's jaw formed a hard line, and one hand clenched into a fist. "At least you're starting to tell the truth now."

"I didn't mean it like that." She waved her hand as if she could dispel all the tension between them—only, it wasn't the sexual kind this time. "Wyatt is in real danger and not from me or his father."

"Yeah, yeah, Jaycee is an unfit mother."

"I'm not even talking about Jaycee." Another car roared past, and a shower of dust peppered her face.

"Can we please sit in the car and finish this discussion?"

"With your gun?"

She smacked her palm against her forehead. "Take the damned thing. I told you. It's in my purse. You can even point it at me if it would make you feel better. Wyatt needs the AC."

Nash opened the driver's-side door and motioned her to the back. "Get in the passenger side. I'll take your purse. Do not try anything."

"With Wyatt in the car?" She stalked around the back of the car and dropped into the passenger seat.

Nash had her gun in his hand and was unloading it. He poured the bullets from his palm into the cup holder. Stroking one finger along the barrel, he said, "Nice piece."

"Thank you." She cranked her head around and wiggled her fingers at Wyatt. "Do you even know why Jaycee dropped off Wyatt with you? Did you even ask?"

"I didn't talk to her."

"What?" Her voice squeaked, and she cleared her throat. "Did she just hand off the baby and you took him with no words exchanged?"

"Jaycee left Wyatt on my porch when I wasn't home."

"Oh, that's rich." Emily slapped the dashboard. "She abandoned her baby on your front porch?"

"She knew I was in town. She knew when I was coming home from work, and she timed it perfectly."

"Oh, that makes all the difference in the world. Do you see why his father might be concerned?"

"Do *you* know why she left Wyatt with me?"

"I do. Two men…thugs, paid Jaycee a visit in Phoenix. They were looking for her boyfriend, Brett Fillmore. Do you know him?"

"The name sounds vaguely familiar, but there are a lot of men in Jaycee's orbit."

Was Nash one of them?

Wyatt started fussing in the back seat, and Emily reached over and turned on the engine. "He needs the air-conditioning."

"He needs his toy." Nash reached onto the floor behind him and plucked up a multicolored stuffed caterpillar. He waved it in Wyatt's face and allowed the baby to grab it from his hand.

"Why were these guys looking for Brett, and what makes you think they were criminals?"

Cocking her head, Emily pursed her lips. "You know I was a cop. Give me a little credit here."

"Okay, why Brett?"

"Brett is involved in drugs—taking and selling. He must've crossed these guys or something and then disappeared. They were sniffing around Jaycee to see if they could get a bead on Brett, and they saw the baby."

A muscle twitched in Nash's jaw. "What did Jaycee tell them about Wyatt?"

"That he belonged to her roommate. Your friend might be a flake, but she's street savvy. She knew why they were asking about the baby."

"But if the baby's father is…your client and not

Brett, why didn't Jaycee just tell these guys? Get them off the baby's case."

"Probably for the same reason I didn't tell them. If she admits Wyatt is hers, they take him and maybe her, too, to force Brett's hand. Also, Jaycee was a side piece. My client has not admitted his paternity yet, and he's a married man."

"Sounds like a prince." Nash ran a hand across his mouth. "Wait, for the same reason you didn't tell them? You've met these guys? These drug dealers?"

"I've met one of them. He's here in Paradiso…and last night he threatened me."

Chapter Eight

Nash's blood thrummed in his ears. This situation just kept getting worse and worse.

"Threatened you? Where?"

"When I got to my motel last night." Emily rubbed her midsection. "Shoved a gun in my ribs, punched me in the kidney, and told me if I didn't turn over Wyatt today at about one o'clock, he'd kill me, you and Denali."

Nash ground his back teeth together. "He knows where I live? He knows who you are?"

"This is what I figured." Emily held up her hand and ticked off her fingers with each theory. "They followed Jaycee here to Paradiso and your house, just like I did. They were watching the house but didn't want to make a move because they found out you were Border Patrol, and they saw me coming in and out with Wyatt. They put a GPS tracker on my car and followed me to my motel, where the one guy accosted me."

"You're telling me there's a GPS tracker on this car right now?" Nash glanced at the side mirror and the time on the dashboard. They'd be expecting her and

Wyatt in just over an hour, unless they saw that she was on the move.

"I took it off and dropped it in your driveway. As far as they know, I'm sitting at your place getting ready to turn over Wyatt."

Nash studied Emily's face, a slight crease between her eyebrows but calm. No wonder she came across as Mary Poppins. The woman had things under control—or thought she did.

"So, you see why I took Wyatt? I was trying to protect him." She folded her hands in her lap and twisted her fingers. "I—I left you a note on the counter explaining things. I wouldn't have just taken off without giving you some kind of...goodbye."

Nash squeezed his eyes closed and pinched the bridge of his nose. "You're not protecting Wyatt, Emily."

"Of course I am. Even though my client isn't expecting me to bring Wyatt to him, once I do, he can keep his son safe." She flicked her fingers in the air. "I'm sure he'll work out some sort of custody arrangement with Jaycee. He's not going to cut her out of Wyatt's life completely."

"Why isn't your client aware of the situation? Why doesn't he know that you're bringing his son to him?" Nash twisted his head to the side and pinned her with a stare.

"He hasn't responded to my texts yet. He's a busy guy, and I'm sure he trusts me to make the right decisions."

She at least had the self-awareness to blush. The reasoning that had been going through her head for the past few days must've sounded even more absurd when she said it out loud in the small confines of the car.

"So, a man who's paying you big money, tens of thousands of dollars, to follow his son and keep him safe is not monitoring or answering texts from you?" He snorted, a restrained sort of sound compared to the screaming in his head. He'd been so impressed with her detective skills up to this point.

"You don't know this guy..." Her voice wavered. "How do you know what he's paying me?"

"I do know this guy, Emily. I just spent quite a bit of time with his finances this morning." He drummed his fingers on the steering wheel. "How do you think I discovered your real identity? You did a hell of a cover-up job—employment history, references, driver's license, a little social media. Helluva job, Officer Lang."

"Stop—" she held up one hand "—calling me that. You can't possibly believe Marcus Lanier is involved in the drug trade."

He narrowed his eyes. "You *do* know what I'm talking about."

"Okay, look. I hacked into your personal email account and I saw his name listed on some spreadsheet, but I thought maybe he was a donor or something."

"I guess he is—a money donor to you and a sperm donor to Jaycee." He hit his fist on his knee. "That's really what you thought, or is that what you wanted to believe as long as he's throwing the money your way?"

"I had no idea, and I still don't believe it." She plowed her fingers through her hair. "He's an important figure in Phoenix. His wife is on all the charity boards. They're movers and shakers."

"His wife, Ming Lee Hong, is from a criminal family in China. She's no angel."

"Wait, wait. Even if Lanier is involved in the drug trade, and I'm not convinced, how does that cancel out his concern for his son?" Lifting her shoulders, she spread her hands. "Bad guys are fathers, too, concerned fathers."

Nash tapped his head. "You're not connecting the dots, but you weren't a cop long enough to make detective, were you?"

She tossed her hair and shot him a glance from her green eyes that looked almost…predatory. "What dots?"

"Let's for the sake of argument agree that Lanier is involved with the cartels. You don't think it's coincidental that he's following a baby that one of the cartels is following? That his so-called mistress, Jaycee, also happens to be involved with a man, Brett, who has drug associations?"

"Are you saying that Lanier sent me *and* those two thugs after Wyatt? For what? Insurance?"

"I don't know, yet, Emily, but think about it. It's too coincidental. If I didn't know what I do about Marcus Lanier and his connections, your story might make sense." Nash wrapped his fingers around the steering wheel. "I could understand a man wanting to keep tabs on his son if he felt the mother was unreliable or negligent and even waiting to get paternity results before making a move, but Lanier?"

"What possible reason could Marcus Lanier have for hiring a PI to follow a baby that's not even his?" She pressed her fingers to her temples.

"Same reason two members of a drug cartel are after him."

"To get to Brett?" Her eyes popped open, and she took a quick glance at Wyatt in the back seat, gnawing on the corner of his caterpillar. "But why use me to do it if you've got a couple of violent gofers ready to do the deed?"

"For the same reason those violent gofers, which has me picturing rabid, bucktoothed animals, didn't strong-arm their way into my house. How much more civilized and less upsetting for a pretty, young nanny to abscond with the baby. It's still a crime, but not a crime that can be attached to him."

"Until I tell the authorities I was working for Marcus Lanier."

Nash met her wide eyes and then dropped his gaze.

"What?" She grabbed his arm. "What's that look?"

"If Marcus Lanier is who we think he is, he's a very dangerous man. He could be setting you up. He could have plans for you."

She crossed her arms, rubbing her skin. "You're freaking me out."

"We have to get Wyatt to safety." Nash tapped the clock display on the dashboard. "It's almost your meeting time. Your buddy is going to come after you when you don't show up at the appointed time."

"I could've been more than halfway to Phoenix by now."

"Halfway to Marcus Lanier." Nash reached around and tugged on Wyatt's bare foot. "Let's get him out of here. The AC isn't even cold anymore."

"Your truck?" She jerked her thumb over her shoulder.

"Can I trust you not to go speeding off to Phoenix?"

"You can trust me." She held up two fingers. "Scout's honor."

"Let's get back to my place. We can leave your car there and we'll take my truck out of town, just to get some breathing room." He snapped his fingers. "Better yet, we can pick up that GPS tracker in my driveway and attach it back to your car. I can have my buddy drive the car somewhere, down to the border, to buy us some time."

"What about Denali?"

"I'll ask him to take Denali, too. His girlfriend has looked after him before, so the dog will be fine with them."

"Would your friend do all that for you?"

"He owes me a couple of favors." Nash grabbed her purse and pinned it between his arm and body. "I'll take this. Follow me back to my place—and don't even think about ditching me."

"I won't. I think this plan will work...for now."

Leaving the keys in the ignition, Nash exited Emily's vehicle and strode back to his truck. He made a U-turn and watched in his rearview mirror as Emily followed suit.

Did she really not know Lanier's character? Why would she? Nobody else in Phoenix did. He was friendly to law enforcement and donated to fund-raisers and other causes. He had all the trappings of a smooth, sophisticated SOB. Emily couldn't see past that? Nash shook his head. She didn't want to see past it.

She'd been fired from her job with the PD and had moved out west to start fresh. Getting your foothold in as a private investigator in a new city couldn't be easy, and doing a job for Marcus Lanier would look good on her résumé. She'd been willfully blind.

He put on his left turn signal just to make sure she remembered the way to his house. As he made the turn, she followed and he blew out a breath.

He pulled his truck just inside the gate, but not too far, as he didn't want to crush the GPS in the driveway.

Emily parked behind him and went around to the passenger side to collect Wyatt. As she approached him, she held out the baby, legs dangling beneath him. "Take Wyatt. I'll get the tracker."

Wyatt whined in his arms, and Nash patted his back. "I know, buddy, but she's all we got right now."

Emily returned with her hand held out and a black device in the center of her palm. "Here it is. We're putting it back on my car?"

"Let's make a trade." He peeled Wyatt from his shoulder. "Get this one a bottle, and I'll secure the GPS to your rental and call my friend. Then I'll throw a few things in a bag and we'll hit the road."

Emily scurried into the house with Wyatt, and Nash got busy. His friend Kyle, who was in security, was more than happy to take Emily's car out to the desert. He was going to have his girlfriend, Meg, follow him in her car, and they'd abandon Emily's rental near the border.

By the time Emily returned with Wyatt clutching a bottle, Nash had settled everything. "We're good to go. Let me just pack an overnight bag."

He threw some things together, his only thought to get away from Paradiso for a day and make a plan. If Jaycee came back here and he was gone, it would serve her right. If she ever turned her phone back on, he could leave her a voice mail. She had to know these guys were after her, or that someone was after her. She wouldn't have dropped Wyatt on him, literally, if she hadn't known. Did she go off in search of Brett? Was Brett Wyatt's father? Was Lanier? Had Jaycee even had an affair with Lanier? Too many questions, no answers.

He burst from the house, holding his breath until he saw his truck idling at the foot of his driveway, Wyatt strapped in the back. He still didn't completely trust Emily.

He rapped on the window of the driver's side and she powered it down. "Let me drive. I know this area better than you, and I have an idea."

She scrambled from the truck and went around to the passenger side with no argument, and he slid behind the wheel and repositioned the seat. "How's our guy doing back there?"

"Happy with his bottle. I think he's sleepy and probably confused."

"That makes two of us." Nash shifted into gear and pulled away from his house.

Emily turned away from blowing kisses at Wyatt and

tucked one leg beneath her. "He really is a good baby, isn't he? He hardly ever cries. That's not normal, is it?"

He lifted one eyebrow. "You really don't know anything about babies, do you?"

"It's amazing what you can learn from online videos, but Wyatt did seem to take to me, didn't he? Babies aren't much different from dogs. Dogs always seem to know exactly who isn't thrilled with their presence and then glom on to that person."

"So, not only do you not know much about babies, you aren't particularly thrilled with them?"

"I wouldn't say I dislike babies." She shook her finger at Wyatt. "Don't listen to this, Wyatt. I've just never been around them much. I don't have siblings, and my dad was too paranoid to allow me to babysit when I was a teen. Only one of my friends has a baby, and I don't see much of her."

Nash placed his hand on her shoulder. "I'm sorry about your father. I read some news articles about his murder."

She blinked and grabbed her sunglasses from the console. "Thanks."

"You got fired from the same department he served?"

"Yeah." She shoved her glasses onto her face. "Where are we going?"

She'd been more forthcoming as Emily O'Brien. Nash cranked up the air-conditioning. "I thought we'd head out to Tombstone, get lost among the tourists. Something tells me you didn't actually do any sightseeing down here."

"You would be correct. In fact, I haven't been to

Tombstone since moving out to Arizona, and I always meant to go." She formed her hands into two pistols. "I wanna see the shoot-out at the OK Corral."

"They do a re-creation of that. It's all kinds of kitschy, but they do a good job of recounting the history of the town in all its violent, bloody glory."

"That's for now." Emily pinned her hands between her bouncing knees. "How are we going to shake these guys?"

"We'll figure out something. When Jaycee returns, I'm going to convince her to go to the police—regardless of what happens to Brett. Right now, I'm more interested in finding out what Lanier's stake is in all this. Is he really the father? Has he discovered some paternal instinct for his girlfriend's baby? What's he going to tell his wife?"

"I told you what he told me. He's in the process of getting a paternity test done—thanks to me." She patted her chest. "I was able to get one of Wyatt's bottles for the test."

Nash twisted his lips. "You were spying on and sneaking around Jaycee and Wyatt before you followed her to Paradiso?"

"Y-yes. I was doing surveillance on her for several days before she took off for Paradiso." She crossed her index fingers, one over the other, and held them out. "Don't crucify me. I thought I had an up-and-up job, helping a father protect his son. That may still be my mission. You don't know for certain that Lanier is involved with the cartels."

Nash ran his tongue along his bottom lip. "Question

for you. Whose idea was it to collect Wyatt's DNA? Yours or Lanier's?"

"It was his idea. He wants a DNA test done first, and then a more formal paternity test once he makes his claim."

"Is he sure Wyatt is his and not Brett's? How can he be certain?"

"Brett didn't come into the picture until later when Jaycee already had Wyatt."

"Are you sure? You got that info from Lanier, right?"

"Yes. I didn't have any reason to suspect or doubt him—and I still don't. Why in the world would a man like that want a baby?"

"Didn't we just go through this? He could want Wyatt for the same reason those two men want him. He knows he's Brett's child and they want to use him as bait."

She shoved her fingers beneath her sunglasses, covering her eyes. "I don't know. I'm confused, but I can get some clarity if you know people."

"Know people?" He cranked his head to the side. "What kind of people? What kind of clarity?"

She'd been cleaning her sunglasses on the corner of her shirt, and she waved them back at a sleeping Wyatt. "Well, we have his DNA…and I have Lanier's DNA, too."

Chapter Nine

Nash swallowed hard and said, "Not sure I want to know how that happened."

"His straw." She rolled her eyes. "I have a straw he used, and I put it in a plastic bag."

"Does Lanier know that?"

"No."

He glanced at her profile, her chin firm. "Why did you take his DNA? It must've been because you didn't trust him. That's it, isn't it? You got a bad feeling from him." He wiggled his fingers in the air. "It was that cop sense."

"I can't tell you why I did it." She slumped in the seat and wedged one sandal against the glove compartment. "Stop calling me a cop. I'm not a cop. I'm a PI."

"What happened to your career in law enforcement? Your father was a respected homicide detective at the same department."

"I thought you did a dossier on Emily Lang and knew everything about me." Her bottom lip quivered, and he had a strong desire to press his mouth against hers.

He snorted instead. "I know almost nothing about

you. I'm assuming most of what you told me was lies. You slipped up by mentioning your father the homicide detective *and* by using your real first name. Seeing Emily Lang in Lanier's financial records wouldn't have even been a blip on my radar if I hadn't just met another Emily."

"And if that other Emily hadn't snooped in your email. You figured that out, didn't you?" She rubbed the tip of her nose.

"I did, but you had me fooled with your act." He clamped his mouth shut, and his lips formed a thin line. She'd fooled him. Used him.

She ran her knuckles down the side of his arm. "It wasn't all an act, Nash. I've really come to care for... Wyatt over these past few days. I'll admit I saw him as a pawn, a piece in a job for a client, but now I'd do anything to protect him—and not just for a paycheck from Lanier."

Puckering his lips, Nash blew out a breath. "What do you plan to do with Lanier's DNA?"

"Ah, this is where your people come into play. Do you have access to Rapid DNA? I'd like to do my own test to find out if Lanier is, in fact, Wyatt's father. If he's not—" she placed a hand over her heart "—then he must want Wyatt for some nefarious purpose, and I'll do anything in my power to stop that."

"Rapid DNA." Nash drummed his thumbs against the steering wheel. "We do use it. We used it in the case of one of the decapitated women last month."

"Having that piece of information about Lanier and

Wyatt could tell us a lot." Emily tapped on the glass. "We're getting closer. There's a sign for Boothill."

"Yeah, except Wyatt Earp is buried out in California."

"Wyatt." Emily turned in her seat and ran a finger over Wyatt's chubby thigh. "Do you think Jaycee named her boy after Wyatt Earp?"

"Could be. Jaycee Lemoin moved to Paradiso right before high school, and she and my sister became fast friends. She was always wild and kept dragging my sister into mishaps."

"Were you a little in love with her?" Emily glanced at him out of the corner of her eye, twirling a strand of hair around her finger.

Nash threw back his head and laughed. "God, no. Jaycee was an annoyance just like my sister, but my sister had her head on straight. Jaycee could lead my sister into almost any harebrained scheme, but my sister drew the line at drugs. She put her foot down for that, and she and Jaycee drifted apart because of it."

"Good for your sister." Emily flicked her finger at his phone, which buzzed twice. "Do you want me to look at your texts, or no?"

"That's my personal phone. You can have a look. Unlike some people, I have nothing to hide."

She plucked his phone from the cup holder and swiped. "Password protected."

He held out his hand and she smacked it into his palm. He entered his passcode with his thumb and dropped it in her lap.

She tapped the screen. "Your friend parked my car

near the border and drove back to Paradiso with his girlfriend."

"Hopefully, those thugs think you took Wyatt over the border. Can you please text him a thanks back?" He flipped his turn signal. "We'll find a place for tonight. There aren't many hotels in town, but most visitors stay in Tucson or even Phoenix and drive down. I think we should be able to find a room."

She turned in her seat and rested her chin on the headrest. She blew kisses in Wyatt's direction and said, "Who could resist this little guy?"

A smile tugged at Nash's lips. That was one thing he hadn't mistaken about Emily. She did care for Wyatt. "Not all the guests are going to be happy when he breaks into a crying fit in the middle of the night."

"He doesn't do that." She pinched Wyatt's toes. "Do you?"

"Yeah, you've never been with him during the night. He does wake up sometimes, but he'll usually go right back to sleep after a bottle."

"Of course he does." She righted herself in her seat and powered down the window. "Do you think the hotel will have a crib?"

"I hope so." Nash scratched his chin. He hadn't thought about the sleeping arrangements. He hadn't thought about a lot. Just wanted to get Wyatt out of Paradiso and away from the danger. But in what direction did safety lie? Surely not in the direction of Marcus Lanier?

They drove past Boothill and the road curved into Tombstone. The center of town where the tourist attractions and performance groups resided still had wooden sidewalks and dirt roads, but cars didn't venture into the center of town. Horse-drawn buggies ruled the road.

He drove past the town's museum and pulled into the driveway of the one hotel he knew had decent rooms. He ducked into the back of the truck and unlatched Wyatt's car seat from its base. Swinging it beside him, he strode into the small lobby of the hotel with Emily leading the way.

Emily tapped the bell at the front desk and a woman dressed in frontier garb poked her head out of the back and said, "Howdy."

Emily pressed her lips together, suppressing a smile. "Hello. Do you have a room for one night?"

"I'm sorry. I don't. I'm actually surprised because July is not typically a big month for tourists—too hot."

"Oh." Emily turned to Nash, scrunching up her face. "What now? Did you say there were a couple of hotels here?"

The pioneer woman interrupted, "I'm afraid the other hotel is full, also, but my friend has an Airbnb not far from here and she loves babies."

"Do you know if she has a vacancy?" Nash raised his brows at Emily, and she shrugged.

"She does, unless someone booked with her in the past hour. I was just talking to her." The helpful woman raised one finger. "Give me a minute and I'll call her for you."

Nash set Wyatt's car seat on the floor, and Emily

crouched before the baby to make faces and grab his feet to bicycle his legs.

The hotel clerk picked up her phone and touched the display. After a few seconds, she said, "Cora? This is Teri. I have a young couple here with a baby, and they're looking for a room. Do you still have one of yours available?"

Young couple with a baby? Not quite. Nash opened his mouth to explain they'd need separate beds, but Teri burst out in her loud voice. "Perfect. I'll send them right over."

Teri ended the call and hunched forward on the counter, folding her hands. "She has one room left, out of three, and she has a crib. You'll have to book the room through the website, but she's holding it for you."

Emily popped up. "Thank you so much, Teri. We've been driving all day, and my husband is a big fan of Wyatt Earp and has been looking forward to visiting Tombstone for a long time."

That fabrication came easily to Emily's lips. Too easily.

Teri's cheeks shone like polished apples as she tucked a strand of gray hair that had escaped from her long braid behind her ear. "So happy to help."

She slid a piece of hotel paper across the counter and scribbled on it. "Here's her Airbnb and the address. You two enjoy."

After Nash had lifted his jaw from the floor, he grabbed the car seat and exited the hotel while Emily clutched the piece of paper.

When they stepped into the heat, he tapped Emily's

arm. "Why did you lie in there? All that stuff about your husband and how I was a Wyatt Earp fan?"

"Why not lie? Why not play the happy couple on vacation with their baby? If someone comes looking for us—now or later—we might as well cover as much as possible. Yes, there was a couple here with a baby, but they were tourists. You know, cover our tracks."

"Is this Private Investigating 101?" He tugged on a lock of her hair, on fire from the sun. "You're a redhead. An unforgettable redhead."

She tilted her head and dragged her sunglasses down her nose, where they perched on the tip. "You think so?"

"I mean—" heat surged across his chest "—not many people have red hair. All anyone has to do is ask if the woman with the baby had red hair."

"You have to at least try. Doesn't hurt to throw a few lies out there."

Nash aimed the key fob at the truck and unlocked it. "Maybe you're in the wrong profession. You lied to me, but you included just enough truth that I discovered your identity. Not that clever."

"Ugh, don't say that. This is my new profession, and I'm going to stick with it." She opened the back door for Wyatt's car seat.

In less than thirty minutes, they had checked into the Airbnb, which was actually a small cottage behind the main house, and secured a crib in the corner.

As Emily crouched next to Wyatt on the floor of the room to change his diaper, Nash eyed the king-size bed. Emily hadn't blinked an eye when their hostess, Cora, had ushered them into the room with the lone bed.

He chugged down half the bottle of complimentary water and then grinned at Wyatt kicking his legs in the air. Wyatt could be their guardian. Parents with babies didn't have sex, did they? That would be too weird, trying to make the moves on Emily with Wyatt across the room in his crib.

Staring at Emily through half-closed eyes, Nash swirled the water in the bottle. Not that Emily wanted his moves. Maybe the undeniable heat was all on his side. Hell, she'd duped him without a second thought and was getting ready to kidnap his friend's baby.

He needed to keep her close.

She glanced up from her diapering duties and her eyebrows shot up. "What? You look like you're ready to interrogate me."

"Would it do any good?"

"What?"

"Never mind."

Emily snapped Wyatt's onesie into place and scooped him up. "Can you feed him while I wash my hands? We might as well do some sightseeing while we're here. I wasn't lying when I said I wanted to explore Tombstone. It'll get our mind off more unpleasant things right now and maybe lead to some fresh ideas later."

"That sounds good, but Wyatt's not the only one who's hungry. I missed lunch, so let's get some food before we see any shows or go to the museum."

"I'm on board for that."

Nash swung Wyatt into the truck and snapped him in place. "You ready to learn about another Wyatt?"

After sharing some pizza at a noisy restaurant, they

spent the rest of the afternoon watching a show in a re-created saloon that involved some of the more colorful historical figures from Tombstone and the OK Corral gunfight. A few times, the loud pops from the guns would set Wyatt off, and Nash would rush outside with him to allow Emily to see a show he'd watched plenty of times.

During the last break, Wyatt had made it clear he preferred being outside, so Nash bounced him in his arms as he walked back and forth across the wooden sidewalks.

As the show let out, Emily poked her head outside the saloon and then waved when she saw them.

She practically skipped toward them. "I loved that. So fun. I had someone take my picture with two of the gunslingers in the show."

Wyatt giggled and clapped his hands, and Emily clapped her hands back. "You missed a great show, Wyatt."

Nash poured the baby into her arms and she hugged Wyatt close, burying her face in his hair. "He probably needs a nap. Do you want to go back to the room?"

"Yeah, I want to check my messages. I got a couple of calls from a fellow agent but no voice mails."

They drove back to the Airbnb and nodded to their hostess on the way to their room. Wyatt was half-asleep in Emily's arms by the time she got his bottle ready.

While she sat in a chair by the window, Nash called Valdez and left a message. "Hey, I saw you called a couple of times. I was busy. Hit me up again."

"Shh." Emily held her finger to her lips. "He's out already."

She spread out his blanket on the bottom of the crib and settled Wyatt on top of it.

Nash's phone buzzed in his hand. "Maybe he's got some news about Jaycee."

"Valdez, you must have something important to tell me."

"I do." The young agent coughed. "You know that body at the border I was going out to investigate today?"

"Yeah?" Nash's heart began to gallop in his chest.

"I hate to break it to you, man, but it's someone you know."

Nash's throat closed up and he couldn't even squeeze out another word. His gaze traveled to Emily, hovering over Wyatt in the crib.

"You there?"

This time Nash managed a grunt.

"It's Jaycee Lemoin. She's dead."

Chapter Ten

The color drained from Nash's tanned face and his body stiffened.

"What's wrong?" Emily pushed away from the crib and sat on the foot of the bed, clasping her hands.

Nash ran a hand over his mouth. "Murdered?"

Emily bounced up. "Murdered? Who? Marcus Lanier? God, not your friend and his girlfriend!"

Nash shook his head at her. "Okay, thanks for calling, Valdez. I'll be back tomorrow."

He ended the call and sat still on the bed, cupping the phone between his hands, his eyes closed.

"Nash?" Emily scooted closer to him on the bed and rested her hand on his thigh. "What happened? Who was murdered?"

Without opening his eyes, he said, "Jaycee."

Emily cried out and covered her mouth. Tears sprang to her eyes and spilled over her lids, creating hot trails down her cheeks until they met the edge of her hand.

A lump formed in her throat and she sobbed, covering her face with both hands. Her shoulders shook.

Wyatt's mother—dead. He'd never know her. Never

remember her. Maybe Jaycee hadn't been the most careful mother, but she loved her boy. Even Emily could see that, although she herself had never felt that love before. Jaycee had loved him enough to leave him with a trusted friend when she felt his life—and hers—was in danger.

Nash rested his hand on her shoulder. "They killed her."

She dropped her hands and reached for him. His sister's friend, the childhood nuisance, murdered.

He wrapped his arms around her and nestled his head in the crook of her neck. He grated out in a rough voice, "I should've done something. I should've protected her."

She stroked the back of his head, his thick hair springy beneath her fingers. "You couldn't know. You didn't know until I told you she was in trouble."

"I should've guessed. Why else would she drop her baby off on my porch? I should've seen that as a desperate move." He drilled his fist into the mattress.

"You tried, Nash. You tried to reach her, but she didn't return your calls. If anyone's to blame, it's me." She pulled away from him and smacked her hand twice against her chest. "I was hounding her just as surely as those two men were. I should've demanded that Lanier take action right away."

Nash, his eyes bright with unshed tears, grabbed both of her hands with his. "Why'd they do it, Emily? Why'd they kill her? If they wanted to get to Brett, they should've taken her hostage to give him an ultimatum."

"Maybe Brett didn't care?" She squeezed his hands.

"Maybe they had her, gave Brett the option of coming in or losing Jaycee, and he chose his life over hers."

"And the baby? And Wyatt?" His gaze tracked over her shoulder to the crib. "My God, he's just lost his mother and who the hell knows who his father is? Some selfish junkie or a possible drug cartel financier? What the hell kind of choice is that?"

Emily flattened her hand against her belly. "Now that they don't have Jaycee, they'll be coming for Wyatt even harder. Maybe that's why they accosted me last night. They'd already killed Jaycee and knew they needed Wyatt. H-how long has she been dead?"

"I didn't ask." Nash wiped his hand across his brow. "I didn't ask much of anything."

"You were in shock." She cupped his face with both of her hands. "I'm so sorry, and I'm sorry I didn't tell you what was going on as soon as I met you."

"You were working for a client." He encircled her wrists with his fingers. "Don't blame yourself."

"But I knew those men were after her, and Lanier wasn't responding to my texts. I should've figured out something was wrong."

"So, we're both going to sit here and blame ourselves for Jaycee's death when the only people responsible are the ones who killed her. Sure, she made some bad choices, but not one of those choices deserved a death sentence. Now Wyatt—" Nash's voice hitched in his throat "—he's an orphan."

"I'm going to have to call Lanier about this."

"Or you can pretend you don't know anything about Jaycee. We haven't publicized her name yet. That story is not going to be released for at least a day. Sit back and see what Lanier has to say. See if he gives away the fact that he knows Jaycee is gone."

"Lanier?" She dropped her hands to his thighs and curled her fingers into his flesh. "You think he had something to do with Jaycee's murder?"

"I don't know, Emily. If he did, that means you're in danger, too."

"After last night, I already figured that, but I have something Jaycee didn't." She pointed to her purse hanging over a chair with her .22 back in its pocket.

"You have something else she didn't."

She raised her eyebrows at him. "What's that?"

"You have me."

"Thank you." She grabbed his arm. "I feel like I brought this danger to Jaycee."

"Jaycee would've been in danger without you...or without me. At least she had the good sense to separate herself from Wyatt."

"Now she's permanently separated from Wyatt." She glanced over her shoulder to look between the slats of the crib at the sleeping baby, unaware that he'd lost his mother for good. "Do you think she found Brett? That's where she must've gone, right? She didn't give you any hint? She must've left you a note with Wyatt along with all those instructions, right?"

"She did." Nash massaged his right temple. "It was brief. Something along the lines of watch my baby for a few days, and here's the baby manual."

"What are we going to do now, Nash?" She clasped her hands, intertwining her fingers to keep from touching him. She wanted to smooth the lines of worry and sadness from his face. "If you hadn't warned me about Marcus Lanier, I'd be headed to Phoenix right now to deliver his son to him."

He met her gaze, his blue eyes still glistening. "You know I'd never allow you to do that—even if I'd never heard of Marcus Lanier. Babies can't be transported around the country by strangers, delivered to people just because they say they're the parents. You understand that, right?"

She lifted her shoulders to her ears. "You mean you have to follow the law, and in this case that means calling the Department of Child Services."

"You can tell Lanier anything you like and maybe he'll even allow you to keep your retainer."

She sucked in a breath. "Is that what you think I'm worried about? Money?"

"Then you agree that we need to contact the proper authorities now? Wyatt doesn't belong to you, he doesn't belong to me and he sure as hell doesn't belong to Marcus Lanier—at least not yet."

"The *proper authorities* don't always make the best calls." She clenched her teeth. "We'll be turning him over to strangers. He knows us. He belongs with us. We can protect him."

"Emily, it's called kidnapping. We can't do it. If we take off with Wyatt and then he's taken from us by force, that'll be a whole lot worse. Think about it."

"I—I see that." She knew her way only led to trouble down the road. Hadn't it gotten her fired? She stifled a sniffle. "Tomorrow? We'll take him back to Paradiso tomorrow and call DCS."

"I'm going to notify the station that we have Wyatt, and I'll have them call DCS. I think that would be safer." Nash scooted past her off the bed and crept to Wyatt's crib. He leaned over and touched one finger to Wyatt's cheek. "What are you going to do about Lanier, Emily?"

"I'm going to try him again today just to test the waters and to gauge if he knows anything he shouldn't. Then tomorrow—" she swung her legs off the bed "—tomorrow I'm going to let him know that DCS has Wyatt because his mother was murdered and advise him to contact DCS to go through the proper channels if he wants custody of his son. And if he wants his damned money back, he can have it."

"You're going to have to make a statement to the police about the man who threatened you."

She opened her mouth, but Nash held up a hand. "You don't have to tell them everything. After all, the guy who accosted you didn't know you had a connection to Lanier, right? He just thought you were a friend of mine who had access to Wyatt. We decided to take a trip to Tombstone to get out of town and heard the news about Wyatt's mom."

He spread his hands. "No covers blown."

"I can do that." She pressed a palm against her forehead. "I'm going to try calling Lanier again. Wish me luck."

She strolled to the window and placed the call as she looked out on a cactus garden in the back of the house. The phone rang three times and then flipped to a message.

She held the phone in front of her and turned to Nash. "I can't even leave voice mail because his box is full. I don't get it."

"Father of the year, unless they got to him, too." He ran a hand through his hair. "Do you mind if we order food in for dinner? I don't feel much like going out."

"I don't feel much like eating. Whatever you like, but that garden out back looks nice. Wyatt will probably want some fresh air when he wakes up."

"He'd like that." Nash sniffed and wiped his nose with the back of his hand.

Emily shoved her phone into the pocket of her skirt. "What's going to happen to Wyatt?"

"As a cop, you should know the drill. They'll contact Jaycee's next of kin, see if she had a will, which I doubt, and try to place him with her family."

"Unless the father steps up." Emily crossed and gripped her upper arms. With Jaycee out of the picture, Lanier would have a clear path to Wyatt. Had he been responsible for Jaycee's death? Had those two men been working for him, as Nash had suggested at the beginning?

"Who is Jaycee's next of kin? Does she have siblings?"

"She may have half brothers and sisters. I don't know. When she lived in Paradiso, she and her single mom rented a house my family owned. Her mother lived with a couple of guys while they were here, and my parents finally had to give her an ultimatum because the men were using and selling drugs from the house."

"Poor Jaycee. No wonder she fell into that lifestyle so easily." Emily dug her fingers into her biceps. Wyatt shouldn't have to repeat that upbringing. "D-do you think her mother will want custody?"

"I don't know, Emily. I hope to God not."

Wyatt stirred in his crib, making mewling noises in his sleep.

Emily said, "I'll get his bottle ready."

"No, let me do it." Nash smashed his fist into his other hand. "I need to do something before I go off and tear this room apart."

Blinking back tears, Emily nodded. Jaycee's death had deeply affected Nash, probably partly out of guilt and partly from childhood memories, but he hadn't been able to let go. She wanted to tell him it was okay if he wanted to cry and let loose. She'd seen her father cry over particular murder cases where he didn't even know the victims, and he'd always seemed more the man for doing so.

But Nash had to deal how he had to deal, and she let him go through the busywork of mixing up Wyatt's formula and warming it up while she hovered over the baby.

Wyatt uncurled his hands and blinked his eyes. His mouth opened for a big yawn.

Emily reached into the crib and rubbed his back. "Hello, sleepyhead. Are you ready for a bottle?"

His unfocused eyes found her face and a smile touched his lips. He recognized her. He was happy to see her standing there. Her heart swelled. Nobody had been happy to see her in a long time.

She slid her hand beneath his body and lifted him toward her. Still sleepy, he nuzzled his head against her shoulder, and she rested her cheek against his soft hair.

The tears came again, silently sliding down her face and running into Wyatt's hair. She choked back a sob.

In a second, Nash was beside her, holding her and Wyatt both in the circle of his strong arms. He bent his head to hers, and his body shook as he cried.

As Nash held her and this motherless child safe in his comforting embrace, Emily's heart filled with a warmth she hadn't felt since the night her father was murdered.

THAT NIGHT, after tacos outside within feet of the cactus garden, Emily put Wyatt to bed in the crib and joined Nash on the patio for a beer.

She rolled the sweating bottle between her hands. "I saw you texting earlier when I was putting Wyatt down. Any more news about Jaycee's murder?"

"No." Wyatt scratched at the soggy label on his beer with his fingernail. "That was Rob Valdez, one of my coworkers. I told him that I would bring Wyatt into the office tomorrow and to notify DCS."

"So, this is it, our last night with Wyatt." Emily traced her finger around the lip of her bottle. "I hope Jaycee's mother takes care of him. I hope he's happy— no matter who he has for a father."

"I don't think it's Lanier. If he told you a true story, he would've been in touch with you as soon as he found out these other guys were after Wyatt. His silence is telling."

"If he isn't Wyatt's father, his intentions from the start were nefarious…and I played right into his hands." Emily took a gulp of beer. "I'm not much of a PI, am I?"

"Even an investigation you'd run on a client wouldn't have turned up Lanier's shady financial deals. We had a forensic accountant working on Lanier, and he's still not sure about the connection to the cartels." Nash eased out of his chair and knelt before hers, sliding his hands up to her hips. "Don't blame yourself. As soon as you explained yourself to me, I believed you. Call me an idiot. God knows, I have plenty of reasons not to trust women, but I knew."

Leaning over, Emily set her beer bottle on the tile and placed her hands on Nash's shoulders. "I'm sorry I tricked you. I really did think I was doing the right thing for Wyatt. I'd seen those men questioning Jaycee and knew they were trouble—trouble coming for Wyatt."

"You did a good job protecting him. You did a good job taking care of him, especially since everything you know about babies comes from online videos."

Her lips turned up on one side, the first time she'd cracked a smile since finding out about Jaycee. "I did okay, didn't I?"

"You did more than okay. You saved me."

She joined her hands together, entwining her fingers behind his neck. "There's something special about us. I felt it from the beginning."

"So did I." Nash's gaze dropped from her eyes to her mouth as his hands moved up to her waist.

She parted her lips, which had started tingling. That ended when Nash pressed his mouth against hers.

She returned the kiss, inching her hands up his throat. With her fingers laced behind his neck, she pulled him closer and he deepened the kiss, thrusting his tongue into her mouth.

She sighed against the kiss and melted into his embrace. Could they make love with Wyatt in his crib? Was that even legal? If not, she'd be willing to break every law to be with Nash Dillon.

Nash's body jerked, and he pulled away from her.

"I—I agree." She put a hand to her hot cheek. "Bad idea."

"Shh." He rose to his feet and turned toward the sliding door that led to their room.

"What is it?" She touched his back, straining her ears for Wyatt's cry.

Nash lunged forward and charged through the door.

With the adrenaline rushing through her system, Emily stumbled after him. She tripped over the sliding door track and screamed as she saw Nash tackle a man hovering over Wyatt's crib.

Nash threw himself on top of the man's skinny frame, shoving his forearm against the man's throat. The intruder bucked and thrashed beneath him, choking out words and foaming at the mouth.

Nash punched the man's face and blood spurted from his beak-like nose. With one knee pressed into the squirming man's midsection, he turned around and ground out, "He was trying to kidnap Wyatt."

Emily yanked her purse from the chair and whipped out her weapon. "Do not make another move or you're dead."

The would-be kidnapper gasped, "Stop. Stop. I'm Wyatt's father."

Chapter Eleven

Nash cranked his head back to stare into the man's face, the high cheekbones prominent, his bug-eyes wild. "You're not Marcus Lanier."

"I'm Brett Fillmore." He held his hands in front of his face. "No more, man. I can prove it. My wallet's in my back pocket."

Emily, her gun clutched in her hand, approached from the side. She leaned over the man, and her gaze scanned his face. "It's him. It's Brett Fillmore."

Brett blinked. "How do you know who I am? Who the hell are you?"

Nash reached for the man's pocket anyway and patted him down after snatching his wallet and throwing it at Emily's feet. Shoving his fingers into Brett's front pocket, Nash pulled out a knife. "I'll take this."

"Hey, a guy needs protection."

Nash pushed to his feet, using Brett's body for leverage. "You're sure he's Brett Fillmore? You saw him before?"

"I did." Emily swept the wallet from the floor and flipped it open, glancing inside and then showing Nash

Brett Fillmore's driver's license. "He was in Jaycee's apartment when I was surveilling it—before she left for the border."

Brett used his elbows to prop himself up. "You were spying on us? On Jaycee?"

Nash narrowed his eyes. "I don't care if he's Santa Claus and Mother Teresa rolled into one. He was trying to kidnap Wyatt."

"You can't kidnap your own son." Brett wiped his arm across his bloody nose. "Can someone help me here?"

Emily responded by leveling her gun at Brett's head. Nash knew there was a reason why he liked this woman.

Her nostrils flared. "How'd you find us here?"

"I know you think Jaycee's a bad mom for leaving Wyatt like that, but she had a good reason and she had every intention of keeping tabs on him." With his eyes on the gun pointed at his head, Brett inched up a little farther to lean against the crib, where Wyatt had awoken and was now crying.

Brett pointed to the car seat in the corner. "Jaycee had put a GPS tracker on the bottom of Wyatt's car seat. Wh-when she didn't show up at our meeting place, I tracked the car seat. I thought maybe I'd find her, too, but when I saw you two instead of Jaycee, I made my move. Can you blame me?"

Nash growled deep in his throat. "Yeah, I can blame you. If you were meeting Jaycee and you knew she was tracking Wyatt, you must've realized who I was."

"Yeah, the great Nash Dillon." Brett hacked up some

blood, spit it in his palm and wiped it on the thigh of his jeans. "I told Jaycee it was a bad idea to leave Wyatt with the cops, but she wouldn't listen."

"Why would that be a bad idea if you're so concerned with the safety of your *son*?" Emily sounded like she was interrogating a suspect, but she did ease off on her aim.

"Because of this." Brett waved a bony hand around the room. "Because you're not just gonna let me have Wyatt, are you? You're gonna play by the rules. I warned Jaycee that her old friend would turn on her in a minute if he thought she was breaking the law."

Emily said, "We don't even know if you're the father."

Brett hit the back of his head against the crib. "Can someone shut him up?"

"Your concern for Wyatt is touching." Nash held up his hands. "I'm going to wash my hands and see to Wyatt. Don't take your gun off him."

"Don't worry. I'm on it."

As Nash washed his hands, Brett blabbed on about cops and Jaycee and his son but never once mentioned Jaycee's murder. Did he know?

When Nash returned to the room, he tossed two towels at Brett, a wet one and a dry one. Then he picked up a sniffling Wyatt and rocked him in his arms. "It's okay, buddy."

"Finally." Brett wiped the blood from his face and hands and held the towel against his nose.

Emily threw Nash a side glance and he dipped his chin.

She cleared her throat. "Do you know where Jaycee is?"

Brett peered at her over the blood-streaked towel. "No. We were supposed to meet in Mexico, and she never showed up. I tried contacting her on her burner phone, but she never responded. That's when I launched the app and the code she gave me for tracking Wyatt. When I saw him here in Tombstone, I made a move."

Emily lowered her gun. "I hate to tell you this, Brett, but Jaycee is dead."

"What? No." Brett shook his shaggy head back and forth. "She can't be. She was supposed to meet me in Mexico. We were going to come for Wyatt together."

"I'm sorry. It's true." Nash patted Wyatt's back as the baby wriggled in his arms. It was as if Jaycee's son had understood what he said.

"Oh, God." Brett buried his face in the towel and muffled cries escaped from the edges. His head popped up, and he said, "It was Marcus Lanier that killed her. I can guarantee that."

Nash studied Brett's face smeared with dried blood. If he'd been crying real tears, the blood would be running down his face again. "How do you know Jaycee was murdered? Emily didn't say anything about that. It could've been a car accident."

Brett's wild eyes shifted to Emily. "Was it?"

"It was murder." Emily slipped her gun into the side pocket of her purse hanging on her body and crossed her arms. "But what made you think that right away?"

"She was being threatened. She told me two cartel guys came by the apartment. She figured Lanier sent them." Brett hunched his narrow shoulders. "That's why she went on the run, and that's why she left Wyatt with you."

With Wyatt nestled in the crook of his arm, Nash sank to the edge of the bed. "What do you know about Lanier? Why would he be after Jaycee? Why would he want her dead?"

"You should know that." Brett swiveled his head between Nash and Emily. "When I told you I was Wyatt's father to stop your attack, you said I wasn't Marcus Lanier. So, you know Lanier thinks he's Wyatt's father."

"But he's not?" Emily's fingers dug into her flesh.

"*I'm* Wyatt's father."

Emily drilled two fingers into her temple and closed her eyes. "Why would Lanier want to claim paternity for Wyatt? He's a married man. Wouldn't it be much easier for him to give up his parental rights when another man is on the scene claiming his paternity?"

"He *thinks* he's Wyatt's father because Jaycee told him he was. They hooked up several times, so it's possible."

"Let me guess." Nash ground his back teeth together. "Jaycee told Lanier he was the father so she could blackmail him. Am I on the right track? Get some cash out of the guy?"

"That's about right." Brett blew his nose on the towel. "You probably know Jaycee better than I do. She told me how your sister was her best friend in high school, and they'd get into all kinds of trouble."

A muscle throbbed in Nash's jaw. "If that's true, you two were playing a dangerous game."

"If that's true—" Emily strolled to the sliding door to the patio, still standing open in the sultry evening, and then spun around to face Brett "—why not just call off the attack dogs? Why not tell Lanier the truth? If he were coming after Jaycee and Wyatt, it's obvious he wasn't going to pay up."

"I told Jaycee to come clean with him. I told her we weren't going to get anything out of him." Brett bunched the towel in his fists.

"And?" Nash switched a fussy Wyatt from one arm to the other.

"She wouldn't listen to me. She said even if Lanier got a paternity test, she had a couple of their hookups on video and she was going to threaten to go to his wife."

"Wait a minute." Emily paced around the room again. "If you believe the two cartel guys who paid a visit to Jaycee before she fled Phoenix were working for Lanier, why didn't they just kill Jaycee then and snatch Wyatt?"

"Are you a cop, too?"

A blush washed across Emily's face, and she put a hand to her throat. "It doesn't matter what I am. You said two thugs went to Jaycee's apartment, and you implied that these guys worked for Lanier. If that's the case, they already believed Wyatt was their boss's baby. They would've had orders then, but didn't do anything. Instead, they left her and the baby alone and put a tracker on her car, just like Jaycee tracked Wyatt and his car seat."

"I'm supposed to understand the mind of a criminal?" Brett jabbed a thumb at his scrawny chest, which had junkie written all over it.

"In fact—" Emily grabbed a handful of Brett's dirty T-shirt and yanked him to his feet "—those criminals seemed a lot more interested in you than Wyatt. Why is that, Brett?"

Brett's eyes widened to the point that his whites surrounded his dark irises. "How do you know that?"

"I was bugging that apartment. I saw all kinds of things." She drilled her finger into his chest. "Those two guys wanted you."

"I don't know why they'd want me instead of Jaycee." He brushed at his shirt where she'd poked him. "But thanks for the tip. Maybe they figured a mother wouldn't use her kid like that, so they thought I was the mastermind."

"Mastermind." Nash rolled his eyes. "We can go around and around all night with this. We'll let the police do their investigation into Jaycee's murder, and we'll let the Department of Child Safety and the family court decide who is Wyatt's father and where he belongs."

"You're kidding, right?" Brett shoved his hands into the front pockets of his jeans. "You're turning my kid over to the system?"

"I sure as hell am not turning him over to you." Nash cuddled Wyatt closer against his chest.

"It's late and Wyatt needs to get back to sleep."

Emily flicked her fingers at Brett. "Get out. If you are Wyatt's father and you want to raise him as your own, you can go through the proper channels."

Brett shoved out his hand. "My knife."

Nash snorted. "Now you're the one who's kidding. Leave, and if you make any more attempts to take Wyatt, I'll kill you."

Brett swallowed hard, his Adam's apple bobbing in his skinny neck. "You'll see. I'm that baby's father and he'll wind up with me—where he belongs."

Emily strode to the front door and flung it open.

Brett backed up through the door, as if he didn't trust them not to jump him. Nash grimaced. The guy wasn't as dumb as he looked.

Emily clicked the door shut after him and locked the dead bolt. "Cora needs a chain on this door. He broke in too easily."

She tiptoed to the bed. "How's our boy?"

"He's almost out. After the commotion, he sensed the tension. It drained him."

"But you calmed him down." She tilted her head. "You're good with him. Do a lot of your friends have babies?"

"Almost none." Nash rose from the bed and settled Wyatt on the crib mattress, holding his breath. "It's kind of like soothing a horse."

"Not quite."

"And you know that how, city girl?"

"He's a baby, not a horse."

"Thanks for that." Nash scratched his chin. "What do you think about Brett's story?"

"I'm going to shut this sliding door before I tell you." She made good on her promise and yanked the drapes across the glass. "He's full of it. Did you notice his crocodile tears over Jaycee?"

"I did. He made a quick recovery. But the story about the blackmail?" He picked up a tortilla chip left over from their dinner and crunched it between his teeth. "That's pure Jaycee."

"Maybe that's why Lanier hired me and then wasn't too upset when I told him those two characters were after Wyatt. He could've even figured out at that point that Wyatt was Brett's son and washed his hands of the whole affair."

"Until Jaycee came back at him with her videos and more demands."

"Until then."

"If that's what went down, then the two cartel guys really were looking for Brett and figured Wyatt was his kid."

"Did they find Jaycee first and try to use her to get Brett to cooperate?"

"If so, that attempt failed. Brett didn't take the bait and they killed Jaycee."

Emily hugged her purse to her chest. "I'm going to sleep with this right next to me in case Brett gets the bright idea to come back."

While he wished Emily would show as much desire to sleep with him as her gun, he crouched before the little safe in the room, where he'd stowed his own weapon. "I've got my bedmate right here."

Emily raised her eyebrows. "You really know how to make a girl feel special."

Placing his gun on the nightstand on the left side of the bed, he chuckled. "I guess that's what happens when you get two cops together."

She opened her mouth, grinned and then snapped it shut. As she unzipped her suitcase, she asked, "What do you think he wanted with Wyatt? He barely looked at him."

"Yeah, I find it hard to believe he has any strong feelings for his son...or his son's mother." He stretched out on the bed and clasped his hands behind his head. "That's a mystery, but I'm sure he's up to no good. You take the bathroom first and I'll put the TV on low."

When Emily retreated to the bathroom, Nash watched images flicker across the TV, but his ears were attuned to every sound from the other room as Emily ran the water and brushed her teeth.

Brett had interrupted a moment between him and Emily that Nash had been anticipating for quite a while, but maybe Brett had provided a warning. Nash and Emily had been so into each other, they'd missed Brett breaking into the room. They had a responsibility to that little boy. They had to get him safely to DCS... and Jaycee's relatives.

Nash kicked off his flip-flops and dragged a pillow into his lap, crushing it against his chest. He remembered Jaycee's mother all too well. That woman had no business raising a child. And the possible fathers? Hell no. Poor kid.

Emily threw open the bathroom door, and he

snapped out of his funk. She'd already witnessed one breakdown, and he wanted to exude the confidence now that he could get both her and Wyatt back to Paradiso safely.

He slapped on a grin. "Did you leave me some hot water?"

"There's plenty." She shook out her T-shirt as she walked to her suitcase to lay her clothes across the top. "Are you taking a shower, too?"

"This town is dusty. I feel like I'm crunching dirt between my teeth." He swung his legs off the bed and grabbed a clean T-shirt and a pair of gym shorts from his bag.

"It is dusty, and I don't care if it is kind of corny, I liked it…until we found out about Jaycee."

He bunched his clothes in one hand. "It was a good day until that."

He slipped into the bathroom, took a quick shower and brushed his teeth. When he returned to the bedroom, Emily was propped up against a pile of pillows watching a comedy.

She patted the bed beside her. "C'mon, I think we can both use a laugh right now."

He dropped his clothes and crawled onto the bed beside her.

She scooted close to him and rested her head on his shoulder. "You're one of the good guys, Nash Dillon."

THE FOLLOWING MORNING, they rose early and had a quick breakfast with Cora before hitting the road back to Paradiso. They left the GPS that had been on Wyatt's car seat in the cactus garden.

Jaycee hadn't been as ditzy as Nash thought. His hands tightened on the steering wheel. She should've taken care of herself as well as Wyatt.

Nash had called in their arrival time to coincide with DCS. They'd hand Wyatt over to a social worker and DCS would find him a foster family until his parentage and Jaycee's wishes could be sorted through.

He was gonna miss the kid…and the kid's nanny.

As they passed Boothill, Nash turned his head toward Emily. "Are you going to contact Lanier as soon as DCS has Wyatt?"

"Yes. If I'm forced to leave a text again, I'll let him know about Jaycee—if it's okay with the police—and that DCS has Wyatt and that he's safe. He can figure out what he wants to do from there, but it's all going to have to be legal and aboveboard."

"Do you think you'll get your final payment, or whatever he owes you?"

"At this point, I don't care. If he turns out to be involved with the cartels, I don't want his dirty money." She slid her sunglasses on and tapped her fingers against her knee, her jaw a hard line.

A good reference from a client like Lanier could've catapulted Emily's PI career into the stratosphere—unless he was a cartel associate and money launderer. What the hell did someone like Lanier want with a baby, even if Wyatt were his son? He must've been trying to foil Jaycee's blackmail attempt.

The drive back to Paradiso went a lot faster than the

drive out to Tombstone, no matter how much Nash tried to delay it. When he pulled into the parking lot of the station, he scanned the cars to see if he could figure out which one belonged to the caseworker who'd take Wyatt away. He swallowed hard when he saw a sedan with a rear-facing car seat in the back.

He threw the car into Park and sat still with his hands resting on top of the steering wheel. Emily sat beside him, staring straight ahead, not moving a muscle.

Finally, she shoved her glasses to the top of her head. "Before we go in, I'm going to change his diaper one last time. I—I don't want them to think he was neglected."

"I'll help you." Nash exited the vehicle and opened the passenger door behind the driver's side. He dragged the diaper bag from the floor of the truck while Emily scooped Wyatt out of his seat.

"C'mon, you little bug. You need to look handsome and healthy to meet new people." Emily's voice hitched in her throat.

Nash's own throat was aching by the time she came to his side of the car with Wyatt in her arms.

She placed him on the diaper mat he'd laid out on the seat and changed Wyatt—one last time. Without hesitation, Nash took the dirty diaper from her and tossed it into the trash can on the edge of the parking lot. He'd come a long way in a few days.

When he came back to the truck, Emily had snapped up Wyatt's clothes and plucked a couple of diaper wipes from the dispenser. She waved one at Nash. "Here you go."

He wiped his hands clean, and then they walked into the station as if they were going to face a firing squad.

When they entered the reception area, four heads swiveled around to watch their progress. Nash narrowed his eyes as he, Emily and Wyatt approached the clutch of people, each with a different expression he couldn't begin to fathom. He could read only Valdez's open face, filled with an almost gleeful humor, but he couldn't understand it. What the hell was so funny about a murdered mother leaving a child behind?

He recognized Detective Espinoza from the Pima County Sheriff's Department and a deputy from the same department and figured the woman for the caseworker.

They'd all been huddled around a computer when he and Emily had walked in with Wyatt. Now their attention stayed focused on him.

Nash coughed, more to get rid of the lump in his throat than anything else. "We have Jaycee Lemoin's baby. I hope you're ready to take good care of him."

The woman shifted her gaze from him to Wyatt, happily lounging in Emily's arms, and smiled. "I'm Alice Daniels, the social worker from DCS. Wyatt looks like a happy boy. We'll do our best for him until…"

Alice jerked her head back toward Nash and dropped her gaze.

Nash exchanged a look with Emily, who shrugged. She felt it, too.

Espinoza nodded to Nash as he lifted the laptop to the counter. "Agent Dillon, we have something to show you."

"I figured you might. You're all acting weird."

As Emily started forward, Alice put her hand on her arm. "May I hold Wyatt?"

"Of course." Emily did the handoff and Wyatt seemed happy with the smiling woman.

Emily slipped a finger through Nash's belt loop and they bellied up to the counter together.

Nash rapped his knuckles on the wood surface. "What is going on? What's on that computer?"

Espinoza spun the laptop around to face Nash and Emily, where a still from a video featuring Jaycee filled the screen. "When we found Jaycee's body, she had a phone on her."

Nash got an adrenaline surge. "Did she capture her killer?"

"No such luck, but Jaycee knew she was in trouble for sure and took some precautions." Espinoza's hand hovered over the mouse. "Are you ready?"

Nash licked his lips. "Yeah, go."

Espinoza clicked the play button, and Jaycee started talking in a video she'd taken of herself.

Her breathy voice with the slight Southern accent she'd picked up somewhere came across the computer speakers.

"So, I know I messed up…big-time, but I love my little Wy more than anything, and I want to make sure he's safe in case something happens to me. This is my last will and testament, and I'm hoping it holds up in a court of law even if I didn't write anything down or get it notarized, 'cause I don't want my mom to get Wyatt." Jaycee pushed her blond hair from her face. "She didn't do such a great job with me. Sorry, Mom, but you didn't. So, I, Jaycee Lemoin, being of sound mind and body do hereby…"

She stopped and giggled, and Nash's heart flipped over.

"Anyway, almost sound mind and body—and that's a joke. What I'm trying to say here is, I want to pick a guardian for my son, Wyatt Lemoin, and I want that guardian to be Nash Dillon."

Chapter Twelve

Nash's mouth dropped open, and he couldn't hear the rest of Jaycee's verbal will over the roaring in his ears. What just happened? Did Jaycee just appoint him, a single man, a carefree bachelor, as guardian for her son?

Emily touched his shoulder. "Are you all right?"

"All right?" He twisted his head to the side and met her gaze. "I'm in shock. I can't… I'm not…"

"You're not locked in or anything, Agent Dillon." Alice the caseworker appeared in his peripheral vision, bouncing a gurgling Wyatt in her arms. "I'm not an attorney, but I've seen a few situations like this. Nobody can force you to take a child, and it's not that easy for one parent to cut out another. If Wyatt's father steps forward, he can fight for custody and a judge will usually go with blood over friendship. Unless…"

Nash snapped his head around. "I'm not Wyatt's father."

Alice asked, "Do you know who is?"

At Alice's question, Emily pinched his side. She didn't have to worry. He didn't plan on getting into the whole sorry mess right now.

"I don't know—for sure." He waved a hand at the laptop, where Jaycee's frozen image beseeched him. "Didn't Jaycee mention the father? Did she give any hints about who was after her or why she was in danger?"

Espinoza shook his head. "Unfortunately, she didn't get into any of that. When I saw that she'd created a video two days ago, I had my hopes up, but all her thoughts were with her son."

Nash braced his hands on the counter, on either side of the laptop, almost nose-to-nose with Jaycee on the monitor. "What happens now?"

"We'll take care of Wyatt." Alice touched her finger to the baby's nose. "Detective Espinoza has already contacted Jaycee's next of kin, and we'll do some research into Wyatt's father. This is all going to have to wend its way through the courts."

"Wend?" Emily stroked Wyatt's leg. "That makes it sound like a long and tortuous process. Wyatt needs his forever home as soon as possible."

"There is a procedure that has to be followed, but we always have the child's best interests at heart. We have many foster families who would take excellent care of Wyatt and treat him as their own."

Emily ducked and picked up Wyatt's diaper bag and kicked her own large duffel on the floor. "These are his things, and we have a car seat in the truck. When are you taking him?"

"Not for a little while yet. I have paperwork to fill out with Detective Espinoza and a few phone calls to make." Alice took the diaper bag from Emily. "He'll be fine here. Agent Dillon, you can decide whether or not you want to take on this responsibility, and then file a petition when we bring Wyatt's case to family court. The mother's wishes on that video and the fact that she left Wyatt with you when she went on the run will both bear strong witness to your claim."

A father? Hell, he never even kept food in the house for himself. Jaycee had dropped off Wyatt with him because she wanted her son protected, not nurtured. Had she believed Wyatt would be in danger even after she died? From whom? What did these people want with a little baby?

Wyatt squirmed in Alice's arms and reached out for Emily.

Emily dropped her head, allowing her hair to create a rosy veil around her face, but Nash spied a teardrop quivering on the end of her chin.

There was no way they could stay here waiting for Alice to take Wyatt away. They might not see him for months. Nash clamped a hand over his mouth. Who was he kidding? Emily would probably never see Wyatt again.

He put an arm around her hunched shoulders. "Maybe we should get some lunch and leave Wyatt with Alice. He'll be fine."

Emily's head shot up and she dashed the back of her hand across her cheek. "A man who claimed to be Wyatt's father tried to kidnap him last night."

Detective Espinoza crossed his arms, resting them on his paunch. "Brett Fillmore?"

"Yeah, has he been around here?" Nash squeezed Emily's shoulder.

"No, but his fingerprints are in Jaycee's car, and we know that because he's in the system. She also has pictures of him on her phone. Let's just say Mr. Fillmore is a person of interest right now. Did he happen to say where he was going after you foiled his kidnapping attempt?"

"No." Nash rubbed his knuckles against his stubble. "He told us he and Jaycee were supposed to meet in Mexico and she never showed. She'd put a GPS tracker on Wyatt's car seat, and Brett followed us to Tombstone."

Espinoza's eyebrows bunched over his nose. "Did he know Jaycee was dead?"

"Said he didn't." Nash shrugged. "I'm not sure why he'd want to kill her, though. Those two were involved in some scams together. We also need to talk about someone else who may be involved in all this. Let me know when you want to interview me."

"Looks like one of those scams got her killed." Espinoza smacked his hand on the counter. "We'll get to the bottom of this, and that little boy will have a good, safe home, whether it's with you, Dillon, or someone else. I'll be in touch. We're still processing items from the crime scene."

Wyatt started to whimper, and Emily cupped his foot with her hand. "It's okay, big guy. Can I hold him for a minute to say goodbye?"

"Of course." Alice handed Wyatt off to Emily, and she held him close, resting her head against his. "It

looks like you two took good care of Wyatt. It's no wonder why Jaycee left him in your care, Agent Dillon."

Emily whispered to Wyatt as she cuddled him, and
Nash blinked his eyes.

Emily gave the baby a final kiss on the head and
held him out to Alice. "Do you need that car seat?"

"No, I have one in my car." As Alice turned to take
Wyatt to the back of the station, Nash skimmed his
hand across Wyatt's back.

"Bye, buddy—for now."

Then he grabbed Emily's wrist. "Let's get lunch.
Espinoza, call me when you're ready. I have a confusing tale to tell you."

"It'll be sooner rather than later, but we're putting
out our feelers for Fillmore right now."

Nash entwined his fingers with Emily's and tugged
her hand. "We still need to pick up your car by the
border."

Emily shuffled her feet beside him, and when they
stepped outside into the dense heat, a sob broke from
her throat.

He drew her into his arms and rested his chin on top
of her head. "That was tough, huh?"

She wiped her nose. "I can't believe how attached I
got to that little boy in such a short time. And he was
attached to me, too, wasn't he? I didn't imagine that,
did I?"

"You were the highlight of his day." Nash kissed the
top of her head. "Do you feel like eating anything?"

"Not really, but I'm not ready to go back to your

place without Wyatt. Does your friend still have Denali?"

"Don't start worrying about Denali, too. The dog is fine." He cupped her damp face with his hands, sweeping his thumbs across her tears. "Wyatt will be fine, too."

"Then why am I so worried about him?" She grabbed his wrists. "It's not just leaving him that broke my heart, but the feeling in the pit of my stomach that Wyatt will never be safe unless he's with you. Jaycee felt that way, too."

"Jaycee brought Wyatt to me because he needed a bodyguard, but a bodyguard does not a father make. She was being sentimental. If my sister, Eve, were here, Jaycee would've left Wyatt with her. Jaycee only ever felt safe in the confines of my family."

"You don't think he needs a bodyguard anymore?" Emily bit her bottom lip and hugged herself.

"He'll be safe in the system. A judge is not going to hand over a baby to some junkie or a shady, money-laundering businessman."

"That leaves you." Emily grabbed the front of his shirt. "You have to take him if you can, Nash. I know it's asking a lot of a bachelor, and one with a full-time career and rodeo fetish, but it has to be you."

Nash raised one eyebrow. "Fetish?"

"You know what I mean." She released his shirt and smoothed her hands over his chest. "Jaycee had her wits about her for once when she left Wyatt with you and named you his guardian."

"It's a big responsibility." Nash wiped a bead of

sweat from his forehead with the heel of his hand. "I'd have to think long and hard about it. Now, let's get to some AC and have some lunch or at least something cold to drink."

He opened the truck door for her, averting his eyes from the car seat in the back. Could he be a father on his own? Emily's presence in their lives had been the only reason the responsibility for Wyatt had seemed easy the past few days. Could he find another Emily?

Before he shut the door, he pinched a strand of honey-rose hair from Emily's sticky cheek and tucked it behind her ear.

Another Emily? Never.

He drove a short distance to a small café, where he and Emily sat across from each other, both slumped in their seats. They'd ordered iced teas but waved off food for now. His hunger clawed at his stomach, but he didn't want to eat while Emily was still in mourning for Wyatt.

As he stirred some sugar into his tea, he asked, "Nothing from Lanier yet?"

"I'd tell you if there were." She spun her phone on the table. "I laid it all out for him in my last text. I told him Jaycee was murdered, DCS had Wyatt and I was officially off the case."

"His silence is strange."

"And I suppose you haven't gotten any more proof that he is involved with Las Moscas."

"I'd tell you if I had. I'm the only one with his file right now—me and Special Agent Webb." He snatched a plastic menu propped up on the edge of the table.

"You need to eat something. I know it's hot out there, but try some soup at least."

She plucked a menu from the stack and ran her finger down the selections. "Tomato bisque."

"Good choice." Nash raised his hand in the air to get the waitress's attention.

When she came over with a refill for their tea, Emily ordered her soup and he asked for a club sandwich and homemade chips.

"Have you contacted your friend about my car and Denali?"

"We texted. He gave me directions to the car, and I'm going to pick up Denali when his girlfriend gets home from work." He covered her hand with his. "Stop worrying about everything. Wyatt is safe and whichever one of those losers is his father, even if he wants Wyatt, isn't going to look too impressive to the family court."

She put her other hand on top of his, creating a stack as big as that club sandwich on the way. "Especially with someone like you in the picture, someone Wyatt's mother named. That has to carry a lot of weight."

Nash avoided the topic of his guardianship. "I'm going to have to tell my sister about Jaycee. Although they weren't close in the end, I know Eve is going to be upset about the news."

"It's hard losing people in your life." Emily gazed into the whirlpool she'd created by stirring the tea with her straw.

"What happened to your father?"

She released her straw and it continued to swirl in

the glass. "He was chasing a murder suspect—the East Side Strangler. They'd gone to the guy's apartment, and he slipped out the back. My father gave chase, and the man turned and shot him."

"I'm sorry. Did the police catch the killer?"

"He died in another shoot-out—suicide by cop. That guy was not going in as a cop killer." Anger flashed from her green eyes, replacing the sadness.

Progress.

"And you followed in your father's footsteps."

"For a while, as you discovered." She pulled back from him as the waitress delivered their food.

As he sliced his sandwich in two and took a big bite, she kicked the toe of his shoe. "You're starving. You didn't have to hold off because of me. Did you think I'd tag you as insensitive if you ate after leaving Wyatt?"

"Exactly." He wiped his mouth with a napkin and pinched a thick chip between his fingers and held it out to her. "Try one."

As she crunched into the chip, he asked the million-dollar question. "What happened to your career as a cop? You got fired, didn't you?"

"For going above and beyond." She shrugged and plunged her spoon into the steaming soup.

"When a cop says he…or she is going above and beyond, that usually means trouble." He pointed a salty finger at her. "Tell me, Officer Lang, what trouble did you cause?"

"The only trouble I caused was for the other suspect in my father's murder who got off scot-free."

"There was another suspect?" Nash pulled a piece of bacon from his sandwich and stuffed it in his mouth.

"He was the guy's cousin. He warned him that my father and my father's partner were coming. He gave the killer an opportunity to get the jump on my father, which in turn led to my father's death."

"He was never charged?"

"No." Emily transferred her whirlpool activity from her tea to her soup, and red waves of bisque slid over the sides of the bowl. "And I was going to remedy that."

"Oh, boy." He put two fingers on her wrist. "Stop making a mess and eat your soup."

She stopped stirring the soup and tapped her spoon on the edge of the bowl. "You see that? You'd make a great dad."

He dug into his sandwich. Why was she pushing fatherhood on him? Did she figure she could visit him... and Wyatt? He wouldn't mind that one bit, and Wyatt would be over the moon, but he couldn't use a baby to get a woman. If he refused to take custody of Wyatt, which he could do, would Emily drift out of his life?

That poor kid had already been used as a pawn—including by his own mother if Brett were to be believed. He didn't want to accept that Jaycee had planned to use Wyatt as a blackmail chip to get money out of Lanier, but as he'd told Emily, that would be a total Jaycee move.

Emily would have to want to see him for him, whether or not he had Wyatt—and his decision to care for Wyatt was too weighty to include an ulterior motive.

If he did take Wyatt, he'd need a nanny—a real one.

Emily waved her spoon in the air. "What are you thinking about?"

"Nannies."

"That's a good sign." She dragged her napkin from her lap and patted her lips all prim and proper as if she were auditioning as a nanny again. "You're right. This soup is delicious. I may even snag a few more of those chips from your plate."

"Be my guest." He shoved his plate toward her. Her depression over Wyatt had lifted either because he'd distracted her by asking about her father's murder...or because she felt confident in seeing Wyatt again when he took custody of him.

Either way, her return to life dispelled his own sadness. He had to believe Wyatt would be fine—with or without him as his father.

He lightly smacked her hand reaching for another chip. "I didn't know you were going to eat all of them."

She spread her fingers and held them out. "Greasy and salty—my two favorite food groups. I need to hit the ladies' room to wash my hands."

"Go ahead. I'll pay." He swirled his finger in the air. "We'd better wrap this up and go get your car out by the border before it gets dark. We can pick up Denali first, and he can come with us."

"Do you think we might be in danger retrieving that car?" She crumpled a napkin in her fist. "They must've followed their GPS out there, and I'm sure the tops of their heads blew off in unison when they discovered what we'd done."

"That's why I want to go out there before dark, and I'm taking you as my sidekick."

"Wait, maybe you're *my* sidekick."

"I'll be the Doc Holliday to your Wyatt Earp any day, Officer Lang." He saluted.

She didn't even get mad at him this time for calling her Officer Lang. Instead, she gave him a smirk as she scooted out of the booth.

By the time she returned from the restroom, he'd paid the bill and gulped down another refill on his iced tea. "Ready?"

As Emily slid into the truck, she put her hand on his arm. "Do you think Alice has taken Wyatt by now?"

"Probably." He snatched her hand and kissed her fingers. "He'll be fine."

They swung by Kyle's girlfriend Meg's place to pick up Denali, and she handed Nash Emily's keys. "Does this have anything to do with the body found out by the border yesterday?"

"You don't need to know, Meg, but that body?" Knots tightened in Nash's gut. "That was Jaycee Lemoin."

Meg covered her mouth with both hands, her eyes wide in her face. "Oh, my God. Does your sister know yet?"

"Not yet. I'll call her later. I doubt she's going to hear this news in New York first."

"I hate to say it…" Meg shook her head. "No, I'm not going there. No matter what Jaycee was up to, she didn't deserve to get murdered."

"I agree." Nash scratched Denali's head as the dog

thumped his tail against his bare leg. "Tell Kyle thanks for me, and I'll catch up with him later."

"Okay. Be careful out there." Meg showed him out and then stepped onto the porch and waved at Emily waiting in the truck. "She's a cute girl. Is this one going to stick around for more than a few weeks?"

"She's not… We're not…you know." Nash bent over to grab Denali's collar so Meg couldn't see the heat wash into his face. He felt like he was back in elementary school.

"Riiight." She slammed the screen door before Nash even made it off the porch.

He let Denali jump into the back seat of his cab, and Nash plopped down behind the wheel.

Denali sniffed the car seat and whined.

Emily twisted in her seat. "I know, boy. We miss him, too."

She undid her seat belt and ducked into the back seat. She popped back up, holding a stuffed caterpillar in her hand. "Oh, no. We forgot Wyatt's caterpillar. It's his favorite."

"I'm sure DCS will have lots of toys for Wyatt."

"Really?" Emily whacked him on the back of the head with the caterpillar, which squeaked. "It's his favorite, Nash. He's going to an unfamiliar place with unfamiliar people. He needs this caterpillar."

"This is not an excuse to get another glimpse of Wyatt, is it?" He rubbed his head. "I thought a clean break would be better."

"I don't even need to see Wyatt. In fact, I'm not sure

I want to, but if we can catch Alice before she heads into Tucson, I'd like to give it a try."

He grabbed his cell phone from the console and made a call to the station. Agent Perez picked up. "Dillon here. Did the caseworker already leave with Wyatt Lemoin? We forgot to give her…something."

"She left about fifteen minutes ago, but you might be able to catch her before she gets to the 10. She asked about a drive-through where she could pick up some food for the road."

"Thanks, Perez." Nash ended the call and dropped the phone in his cup holder. "We'll try to catch up with her before she hits the 10."

Nash navigated to the two-lane road that led to the 10 freeway with a heavy foot. Once Alice got to the freeway, they wouldn't be able to stop her.

He glanced at Emily hugging the caterpillar to her chest, a small smile curving her lips. She'd better not be up to something.

Five minutes of driving and they'd seen just one other car on the road. He took the next curve and eased off the gas pedal as he spotted a white car up ahead. He tapped the windshield. "Does that look like Alice's car?"

Emily hunched forward in her seat and shoved her sunglasses into her hair. "Yeah, maybe, but that car isn't moving, Nash. It's on the side of the road."

"Are you sure?" He squinted through the shimmering waves that pulsed off the scorching pavement and plucked off his own sunglasses. Dusk in the desert could come on fast and create optical illusions.

They drew closer to the white car, and as it got bigger, he realized Emily was right—it wasn't moving. The hair on the back of his neck quivered. "I think that is the car. Maybe she's changing Wyatt."

"In the middle of the desert." Emily shot forward in her seat. "A DCS worker wouldn't do that."

"Unless he got sick."

Emily's hands clenched as she pressed them against her stomach. "Is it crooked? Does the car look like it's parked at an angle to you?"

"Some." Nash slowed the truck and blew out a breath. "She's in the car."

"What's she doing?" Emily had grabbed the handle of the truck as if ready to jump out now.

Denali barked into the tension radiating throughout the truck's cab.

Nash put on his signal and rolled over the gravel on the side of the road, kicking up dust. His heart hammered against his rib cage. "Why the hell is she sitting there?"

Before the truck came to a complete stop, Emily threw open the door. "Something's wrong."

"Maybe she had some car trouble." Nash cut the engine and made a grab for Emily as she slipped out of the truck. "Wait, Emily."

As he opened his own door, Emily scurried to the driver's side of Alice's car. Emily stumbled back, her hand to her chest, her mouth gaping.

Nash charged out of his vehicle and strode toward Emily, his shoes crunching over glass in the road. When he got to the white car, he stared through the jagged glass at Alice sitting upright behind the wheel—a bullet hole in her head.

Chapter Thirteen

Emily huffed air from her nostrils to expel the sickening metallic taste that seeped down her throat, making her gag. She stumbled past Nash and yanked open the back door of Alice's car.

She blinked at the empty seat and dived into the car, sweeping her hand across the leather as if Wyatt's car seat were just invisible. She flung herself forward and buried her head in her arms. "They took him. They took Wyatt."

Behind her, Nash spoke urgently into his cell phone, his words muffled through the pounding blood in her ears.

His hand stroked the back of her calf. "Emily? I called the Paradiso police and Detective Espinoza. They're on their way. Come on out. You might be compromising the crime scene."

Covering her face, she scooted out of the car backward until her feet touched the ground.

Nash curled an arm around her waist and pulled her out the rest of the way. She barreled into his chest, sobbing against his shoulder.

"I knew it. I knew Wyatt was in danger. As soon as he left us, I've been fearing for his safety."

Nash smoothed her hair back from her hot forehead and set her away from him to look into her eyes. "There's good news here."

"Here?" She flung her arm back at the bloody mess in the front seat and the yawning emptiness of the back. "What could possibly be good?"

"They *took* Wyatt. They didn't kill him."

At the thought of Wyatt's death, her knees buckled, and Nash caught her arm. "Think about it. If they wanted to get rid of Wyatt, they could've done so when they overtook Alice and killed her. They didn't."

She rubbed her eyes and cranked her head around to peer into the back seat again—this time to look for Wyatt's little lifeless body. She nodded jerkily, as if someone were pulling strings to make her move, as her muscles seemed frozen.

"But for what purpose? Why did they take him? What are they going to do with him?"

Nash's voice continued to soothe. "They took his car seat. They took his diaper bag."

"They took *him*. Why?" That one word threatened to turn into a wail, so she clamped a hand over her mouth.

"What has Wyatt always been, even to his own mother? A bargaining chip. Not that I trust Brett any farther than I can drop-kick him, but he made the claim that Jaycee planned to use Wyatt to blackmail Lanier. Like I said before, that sounds like a Jaycee move. And those two thugs wanted Wyatt to force Brett to give himself up to them. Lanier wanted Wyatt for some other reason, and that's why he hired you. Was it to find out if he's the boy's father? Was it a countermove against Jaycee?"

Emily doubled over. "I feel sick that he used me. I sold out Wyatt for money. I'm as bad as all the rest."

"Stop that." His hands pinched her shoulders. "You were the one good person Wyatt had on his side."

"And you." She tipped back her head to search Nash's face. "But we gave him up. We had him protected, and we handed him off."

"We didn't have a choice, Emily."

"That's where you're wrong." She twisted away from him. "You play by the rules, but I don't. If it were up to me, I never would've handed Wyatt over to DCS."

"That would've gotten you arrested, and I can assure you that would've been a lot worse than getting fired from a PD. Focus." Nash's head jerked to the side as the sound of sirens pierced the darkening sky. "Wyatt's alive, and he's going to stay that way because he's valuable to the person who took him."

"Who did take him, Nash? The way I see it is that we have three suspects or groups of suspects—the drug thugs, Brett and Lanier."

"I agree. You saw the car the two cartel guys were driving, didn't you?"

"Black sedan, Crown Vic, dark tinted windows, white wall tires, antenna, paper plates on the back."

"Good job. You got all that when you saw the car driving by my house?"

"I thought I might need that information later—and here we are." The emergency vehicles came into view, and Emily gritted her teeth against the cacophony of horns, beeps and sirens. She pressed her hands against her cheeks. "Poor Alice. She was just doing her job. Why'd they have to kill her? They could've taken Wyatt from her at gunpoint."

"Maybe she wouldn't let them. It seems Wyatt had someone else on his side."

IT WAS ALMOST ten o'clock by the time they got through questioning at the Border Patrol station. Denali had been napping in an interview room with a bowl of water and someone's leftover steak.

The Pima County Sheriff's Department had put out an APB for Brett Fillmore, using one of his old booking photos. Every patrol unit had an eye out for a black Crown Vic with paper plates. Detective Espinoza had even put a call in to Marcus Lanier when they told him the billionaire might be involved, and discovered he was out of the country.

Emily, her emotions wrung out, slumped in the passenger seat of Nash's truck, holding Wyatt's caterpillar against her chest. Denali whimpered in the back, but Emily couldn't bear to turn around and see the empty car seat.

Wyatt joined her in the truck and clutched the steering wheel with white-knuckled hands. "It's a good start. We'll find him."

She drew in a shaky breath. "I'm exhausted."

"I know you are." He rubbed her leg. "We're going back to my place, right? There's no way I'm dropping you off at that motel to be on your own."

"I wouldn't want to be."

"Good." He started the truck and veered toward the main drag in town. "And we're eating."

She dropped her chin and pulled at the fabric of her grimy blouse. "I'm not going out looking or feeling like this."

"We do have take-out pizza in Paradiso, believe it or not. I'm going to run in to the pizza joint and place an order for delivery." Nash parked in a strip mall boasting a chain pizza place and whistled through his teeth. "Denali, take care of her."

When Nash slammed the door of the truck and locked it with his remote, Emily pulled her purse into her lap with the gun pocket on top and then reached back and scratched Denali under the chin. "I trust you, boy, but I need extra insurance. Whoever named Paradiso must've been joking."

Nash returned faster than she expected and hopped into the truck. "I ordered us a large with everything on it. They're going to deliver it in about forty minutes."

"I don't think I can eat with Wyatt out there somewhere."

"In one way it's a blessing he's still a baby. He's not going to remember any of this drama when he gets older. We'll have stories to tell." The truck bounced as Nash wheeled out of the parking lot and Emily's stomach bounced with it.

Did this mean Nash was going to accept the conditions of Jaycee's will and adopt Wyatt? If he did… Her thoughts trailed off into some vague, hazy future of Nash raising a son by himself. Where did she fit into that picture?

If Jaycee's mother took Wyatt, Emily would never see him again. If Lanier or Brett got him, God forbid, she'd never know another good night's sleep. It had to be Nash.

They drove through town and made the turn to Nash's place. Emily gripped the sides of her seat. "It seems like we left here so long ago, but it was just yesterday. We thought we were keeping Wyatt safe and we turned him over to danger."

"We didn't know that, Emily. Stop blaming yourself for one minute." He slammed the steering wheel with the heel of his hand. "Stop blaming me."

She grabbed his bicep. "I'm not blaming you. I'm sorry if it seems like I am. I'm just so damned worried about him."

His nostrils flared and he closed his eyes. "We'll get him back. Do you still have that straw with Lanier's spit on it?"

"Yes, why?"

"I wanna know who fathered Wyatt. That can go a long way to tell us motive. If Brett's his father, I can't understand why he'd want to kidnap him. He can't seriously want to be Wyatt's father without Jaycee around to take care of the baby."

"But if Lanier really is the father and Brett took him?" Emily held her breath, her muscles stiff.

"Maybe Brett wants to continue the blackmail scheme he and Jaycee started. Maybe he's going to hold Wyatt over Lanier's head until Lanier coughs up some money." He parked the truck, but neither one of them made a move to get out.

"What if those two goons are the ones who took Wyatt?" She shivered. "They must believe Wyatt is Brett's son. What worries me about that scenario is if that's what happened to Jaycee, then clearly Brett doesn't care about anyone but himself and Wyatt will meet the same fate as his mother once they discover that."

Nash brushed a thumb across her cheek. "Don't go there."

"Are you going to try to pull some strings to test Lanier's DNA against Wyatt's? Because you know the official route will take forever even with a missing baby at stake."

"I'll see what I can do." He jerked his thumb over his shoulder. "Denali is going crazy in here. Let's go inside before the pizza beats us."

When Nash got out of the truck, he had his gun at his waist. Emily strapped her purse across her body ready to be his backup, or his sidekick. Did she want to be more? Was she confusing her feelings for the baby with her feelings for the man who would adopt him?

Nash let Denali have free rein to sniff the porch and the front door as an early warning system. The dog just seemed anxious to get inside.

Nash shoved open the door and stood back, his head held to one side. "I think we're good. Denali's instincts are right on, and right now he just wants to run out back. I've also been checking my security cameras and all has been quiet."

Despite his words, Nash went through the house and kept his gun with him. Satisfied, he slid open the back door for Denali. "Go for it, boy."

Denali scampered out back for a run and Emily collapsed in a deep chair, grabbing the remote for the TV. She clicked it on and immediately regretted it as a picture of Wyatt stared back at her from the local news.

She called to Nash, "They put out an Amber Alert."

"I knew they were going to do that." He took the remote from her stiff fingers. "Let's turn that off and put our heads together. The other possibility we didn't discuss in the car is if Lanier kidnapped the baby and he's the father. Why would he do that?"

A whisper of fear feathered across the back of her neck. "That's the worst possible scenario, Nash. If Lanier's the father and he killed Jaycee and kidnapped Wyatt, it could only be to stop this blackmail attempt. And what better way to stop it than to get rid of the evidence?"

"If that's the case, why not dispose of the evidence right away, at the same time he took care of Alice?"

"If he killed Wyatt right there in his car seat—" she stopped and pressed a hand against her galloping heart "—he'd be leaving the evidence, wouldn't he? Nobody but Jaycee and maybe Brett know Wyatt's true parentage at this point. Espinoza's going to want to find out who Wyatt's father is. If Lanier leaves Wyatt in the car and the detectives find out Lanier is the baby's father, he'll have a lot to answer for."

"Good point, but just because he's the father, it

doesn't mean he'd want to kill the baby." Nash moved into the kitchen and opened the fridge.

Emily snapped her fingers. "He also wouldn't want his wife to know."

"Is that what he told you when he hired you?" Nash held up two bottles of beer in the kitchen. "Beer?"

"Please."

"Glass?"

"No, thanks."

He handed her the bottle and she took a swig before continuing. "When Lanier hired me, he was all concerned parent. Jaycee had told him he might be the father and he wanted to protect Wyatt from her if that were the case. He told me he was hiring an attorney and arranging for a paternity test."

"Touching." Nash raised his bottle and chugged back a few gulps.

"What if that's true, Nash? What if everything Lanier told me is true? What if Brett is lying about the blackmail scheme?"

"If Lanier was being honest, we have one less person to worry about. But that doesn't explain why Brett kidnapped the baby. The only use Wyatt is to Brett is as a bargaining chip, and he wouldn't be much of a chip if Lanier were the happy father."

Emily folded her hands around the bottle. "I wish we would've been more insistent about protection for Wyatt."

The knock on the door saved her from Nash's retort. He snapped his mouth shut and held up his hand. "Food."

Nash returned to the room balancing a pizza box on his palm. "Let's eat and strategize."

She hopped up from the chair and followed him into the kitchen. "Plates?"

He swiped some paper plates from the top of the pizza box. "I had them include the plates and napkins. All we have to do is eat and throw away the trash."

"That's my kind of meal." She pinned a plate to the counter with her index finger as he dropped two slices of pizza piled with meat and veggies onto it. She carried the plate back to her chair and tore the slices apart.

Nash joined her, taking the couch and plopping his plate on the coffee table. "Brett's not going back to the apartment he shared with Jaycee in Phoenix. He knows the cops are after him now to question him about Jaycee's murder and Wyatt's disappearance. Where would he go?"

"I'm trying to think." She pulled a string of cheese from the top of her slice and sucked it into her mouth. "When the two cartel guys came looking for him at the apartment, Jaycee pretended they'd split up. He'd been gone a few days by the time those men showed up, so he probably knew they were looking for him."

"You were bugging the apartment prior to that, right? While Brett was still there?"

"I was."

"Video?"

"Video and sound."

"You saved it?"

"I have it on my phone. I can download it to your laptop." She licked her fingers, although she hadn't yet managed a bite of pizza. Nervous excitement now fizzed through her veins. "He could've mentioned some place, right? A place where he was going to hide."

"That's what I'm thinking. It worked so well the first time. Those guys never did find him. If he did take Wyatt, maybe he headed back to his safe place."

"Yeah, yeah." She bounced on the chair. "They for sure talked about his plans, but I didn't pay much attention at the time."

"Then that's a good start." He wiped his hands on a clutch of napkins and pushed up from the couch. "Let's do that right now."

Emily retrieved her phone while he set up his laptop on the coffee table, next to their plates.

"We can do the download via the Wi-Fi. Our tech guy in the department showed me how to do a bunch of stuff like this." He tapped the table. "Bring up the videos and put your phone here."

She accessed her video files for the dates before Brett left the apartment and read off the file names to Nash, who entered the information into his laptop.

"Voilà." He waved his hand over his laptop. "Now we have entertainment while we eat."

Emily munched on a piece of pizza while hunched over Nash's computer, her gaze following the figures on his display as they moved in and out of Jaycee's living room.

"Whoa, who's that?" Nash leveled a finger at another woman in the frame.

"That's Jaycee's roommate. Jaycee tried to tell the cartel guys that Wyatt was the roommate's."

"They obviously didn't believe her." Nash shook his head. "Did these two fight all the time like this?"

"Pretty much." Emily felt a smile twist her lips despite herself when Jaycee came into the frame from the back carrying Wyatt. "There's our boy."

"I'm going to turn up the sound, but they probably won't say anything important with the roommate there. We can take turns keeping an eye on it."

"You know what's weird?" Emily held her hands over her plate and brushed the crumbs from her fingers. "If they did have this blackmail plan for Lanier, I never heard it."

Nash lifted a shoulder. "Doesn't seem like they talk about much at all—mostly snipe at each other."

"Jaycee had bad taste in men...except for one." Emily crumpled her napkin and tossed it onto her paper plate with her crusts. "You."

Nash finished off his beer and clinked the bottle onto the coffee table. "I'm no prize. I work too much, I prefer superficial relationships and there's that rodeo fetish."

"It sounds like you're trying to warn me off." Emily scooted to the edge of the chair. "And why do you prefer superficial relationships?"

"Because of this." He swept his arm to the side. "This property, this business. My family has a lot of money, and women seem attracted to that."

"How can you be so sure it's the money and not the man?" She assessed the handsome face in front of her, the pure masculinity emanating from the lanky frame that housed a sinewy strength. Was he fishing for compliments?

"Let's just say I had a couple of bad experiences that made me wary."

"You weren't too wary to hire a nanny on the spot in the supermarket parking lot." She swirled the remaining sips of her beer in the bottle.

"There was something about that freckled face I trusted." He hunched forward, elbows on his knees, a light smoldering in his blue eyes. "And I wasn't wrong."

"Ha!" She slammed her bottle next to his. "You couldn't have been more wrong. I was a nanny under false pretenses, and I almost absconded with Wyatt."

"For what you thought were the right reasons. You turned on a dime when I explained things to you." He had inched closer across the table.

"So did you." She wound a lock of her hair around her finger. "For a distrustful sort, you accepted my story pretty quickly, even inviting me to your side."

"Like I said—" he reached across the coffee table and cupped her face with one rough hand "—something about that freckled face I trusted."

Emily parted her lips. Her breath came out in short spurts. "I can't imagine why."

"Neither can I." He pulled her close and slanted his mouth across hers, right over their paper plates, greasy napkins and pizza crusts.

The spicy pepperoni on his lips mingled with hers, and she braced a knee on the edge of the table to dive deeper into his kiss.

He rose to his feet, hitching an arm around her waist to take her with him. Their bodies created an arch over the table, and when she wrapped her arms around his shoulders, she took them off balance.

Nash steadied them and broke their connection. Then he took one long step over the coffee table and took her in his arms properly...or very improperly with the way his hands wandered down to her derriere, cupping and lifting her to fit their hips together.

She sighed against his mouth, and he murmured, "Do you want this?"

This time she broke their kiss to gaze into his eyes, the smolder more like a blue flame now. "There's nothing more I want right now, except..."

He placed a finger against her throbbing lips. "We both want Wyatt back, but I need to know you want me, too."

Did she want him without Wyatt? Would she see him again if he refused custody?

Falling against his chest, she entwined her arms around his neck. "I do want you, Nash Dillon. I wanted you the minute I saw you fumbling with that baby in the parking lot."

He pressed his mouth against hers again, and this time it seemed as if a barrier had been lifted between them.

The kiss scorched her lips, branding her somewhere deep inside, taking possession of her soul. If she had doubts before that she could separate the man from the baby, Nash's kiss torched those doubts and turned them to ash.

He turned around with her in his arms and sank to the chair she'd just vacated, pulling her against him.

She bent her knees and wedged her legs on either side of his hips as she straddled him. She plucked at the hem of his T-shirt and yanked it up and over his head.

Running her hands along the hard ridge of muscle on his chest, she planted a kiss on his collarbone. "Mmm, if this body is the result of your rodeo fetish, I wholeheartedly approve."

He lifted one eyebrow in that sexy fashion he had and said, "Let's see if you approve of my other fetishes."

"If one of those is making love in a recliner, again you have my stamp of approval." She ditched her blouse and tossed it over her shoulder.

Nash unhooked her bra with an expertise that gave her pause, but only for a second, as he took one of her nipples between two of his fingers and rolled it slowly.

She gasped and arched her back.

He bent his head and took her other nipple between his lips as she squirmed in his lap. He caught his breath and slammed his head against the back of the chair.

"You're gonna have to stop moving against me like that. I'm only a simple man."

"Nothing simple about you, Nash, but I'm no tease." She pulled at his fly, undoing the buttons at the top and then yanking down his zipper.

He lifted his hips in all eagerness, and she pulled off his shorts and briefs in one motion. She rubbed her bare thighs against his, and he groaned.

He lifted her skirt and ran his hands beneath her panties, caressing her bottom. He grabbed the edge of her underwear, and she awkwardly rose to her knees and tried to disengage one of her legs from between the chair and his thigh.

"Go ahead, rip 'em. I've got others. Better ones."

"I can reimburse you."

"Don't worry. I'll give you an itemized receipt."

Nash chuckled in her ear, gathered her panties in his hand and gave a quick tug. The lacy material ripped, and she lifted her hips and skimmed her tingling flesh along the tight skin of his erection.

The chuckle in her ear turned to a moan, and he dug his fingers into her backside. He positioned her body so that his tip caressed her wet folds.

In a rough voice he said, "We can take it slower later or if we ever make it to a bed, but right now I want you so much it aches."

She whispered. "I feel it, too. I need you to fill… to fill me up."

Did she need to feel whole after losing Wyatt? She didn't want to think right now.

When Nash plunged into her, she stopped thinking altogether. Her body and mind became a mass of feelings and emotions. She moved against him and up and down, bracing her hands on his shoulders.

She rode him just as surely as he rode those bulls in the rodeo.

He slowed his thrusts and shoved his fingers into the crease where their bodies met. He stroked her flesh. "Tell me how. I want you to reach your climax before I explode inside you."

She had no words. Whatever he was doing at this minute was driving her to a pinnacle she'd never reached before. She just nodded, and he kept caressing her in the same spot, in the same way.

She held her breath as the tension built in her body. She'd stopped moving and her rigid muscles made her feel as if she were ready to shatter.

Then she did shatter. Her climax whipped through her, lashing her over and over. She thrashed her head back and forth, her hair creating a red wave between them as Nash pumped her harder and faster.

Before she even came to her senses, Nash's body stiffened and he drove into her, lifting her to her knees. A red flush spread across his chest and his jaw clenched.

He gave a harsh cry and pulled her in for a kiss as he reached his peak and plunged into her again and again.

She slipped off his lap to the side, one leg still hitched over his leg, her skirt crumpled around her waist, her head on his shoulder. All she could manage was a faint "Oh."

Tracing a finger down her spine, he said, "Maybe we can brush our teeth, bring Denali in and slow this down in the bedroom."

She ran her tongue along her teeth. "I definitely need a toothbrush."

"I'll get the dog." He planted his hands on her bottom and shifted her off his lap. Then he struggled to his feet and crossed the room to the patio door. He stuck his head outside and whistled.

As Emily swept up her tattered undies from the floor, she glanced at the video they'd left running on the laptop. They'd have to backtrack and see what they'd missed while they were otherwise engaged.

The roommate had left and Jaycee and Brett were discussing his departure. Her pulse bumped up a few notches as she pulled the computer closer to the edge of the table and turned up the volume. She listened to their conversation for several seconds, the thumping of her heart almost drowning out their words.

She let out a squeak, and Nash jerked his head up as Denali ran through the door. "What's wrong?"

Jabbing her finger at the laptop, she said, "I know where Brett took Wyatt."

Chapter Fourteen

Nash almost tripped over the dog as he rushed to Emily's side, and he still ended up stubbing his toe on the coffee table. The throbbing pain didn't even faze him. "Whaddya got?"

"Listen to this." Emily dragged the time back on the video and clicked Play.

Nash peered at Jaycee, clutching Wyatt to her chest. "Where will you be?"

Brett winked. "Somewhere no one can find me. One of my mom's husbands had a place in a trailer park. He's dead and gone, but I've used that trailer on and off for years. Nobody knows about it."

"Where is it?"

"Down by the border." He continued giving Jaycee the particulars, but Nash didn't even have to listen.

"I know that trailer park. I wouldn't even call it a trailer park, and it's not official—just a bunch of people who brought their RVs and campers together. These places dot the desert."

Emily bunched her ripped underwear in her fist and pounded her knee. "He must be there now with Wyatt."

"If he has him." Nash stopped the video and shoved the computer back on the coffee table. "We don't even know if Brett has Wyatt."

"He tried to kidnap him from us. That's good enough for me." She swept her bra and blouse from the floor and stuck her arms through the straps.

Still naked, Nash pulled Emily's skirt down around her legs and smoothed the material against her thighs. "Where are you going?"

"We're going to get Wyatt." She grabbed his briefs from the floor and tossed them into the air for him.

Nash caught his underwear and shook them at Emily. "Hold on."

"No, no, no." Emily whipped her head back and forth. "You're not going to tell me that we're turning this information over to the police, are you? Do you think they're going to rush over there immediately and grab Wyatt? They'll need a search warrant at the very least. If they come rolling in with lights and sirens, they'll spook Brett and the other residents."

"Brett Fillmore is a person of interest in a murder and kidnapping. The Pima County Sheriff's Department will do this the right way." His words faltered at the end as he caught sight of Emily's face, her liquid eyes and thin lips conveying both sadness and determination at the same time.

"Please, Nash. We did it the right way when we turned Wyatt over to DCS and look what happened." She grabbed his hands. "Of course, we'll go through proper channels if we find Brett, but let's try it my way this time."

"Your way got you fired from your job." But those shimmering green eyes were already weakening his resolve—and Emily knew it.

"Okay, we'll slow down. I need a shower—" she dangled her lacy panties from her fingertips "—and a change of underwear, and then we're going out there to rescue Wyatt."

They both showered—separately—and changed into dark clothing. If he hadn't made love with Emily, would he be so quick to chuck all his good sense out the window and rush into the desert to confront Brett? He loaded his weapon and clicked the chamber shut. *Guess you'll never know, Dillon.*

Emily strapped her purse across her body, her hand resting against the gun pocket. "How far is this place?"

"Now you ask?" He hitched a backpack containing all kinds of gadgets over one shoulder. "It's about an hour. We head south and then we veer east toward New Mexico. Let me warn you. The kind of people who inhabit these desert compounds are not big fans of law enforcement. They're not fans of outsiders at all. Brett must be known there to feel comfortable, and the inhabitants wouldn't blink an eye if he showed up with a baby."

"Even more reason for us to contact him on our own without the law."

He cocked his head. "Do you think Brett's going to give up Wyatt without a fight?"

"No." She licked her lips. "But from what I saw of him, he doesn't pose much of a threat."

"Really? If he did take Wyatt, he murdered a DCS

worker and kidnapped a baby in broad daylight. Dude may be stupid, but he's got guts and that's a lethal combination for anyone who gets in his way."

Emily widened her stance and crossed her arms. "He has Wyatt, and we're gonna get him back."

He stalked toward her and planted a kiss on her forehead. "I know you mean that, but if I sense you're in any danger, we're pulling out."

"I hear you." She dropped her head to adjust her purse strap, and Nash's gut tightened.

He knew he'd have to physically remove her from rescuing Wyatt in the face of danger, and he wouldn't have it any other way—but he'd be ready.

Nash locked the sliding door to the patio in position with just enough space for Denali to squeeze through it. He set up some dry kibble and water in the kitchen. Scratching the dog behind the ear, he said, "Sorry, boy. Clay is never going to let me dog sit you again when he hears about this."

"But Denali is going to be so happy to have Wyatt back home again." She hugged Denali, burying her face in his fur.

Nash didn't want to ruin the moment by pointing out that even if Brett did have Wyatt and even if they got Wyatt back, they'd still have to turn him over to DCS. Nash was already going out on a limb here. He didn't need to add a charge of kidnapping to the list.

Once he secured the house, he and Emily climbed into the truck. He didn't need the GPS to find the border. He knew every inch of it, and this particular desert outpost wouldn't register, anyway.

He cranked on the engine and said, "We're going to have to hike in. We can't drive a truck up to this site, even after midnight, or *especially* after midnight."

"I'm ready." She wedged a sneaker on the dashboard. "It's a good thing we still have Wyatt's car seat in the truck—not that I'd let a little thing like a car seat stop me from taking him home."

Nash bit the inside of his cheek as he swung around the crescent of his driveway and through the front gate. *Home.* Emily kept using that word. Even if he decided to go through with the custody arrangement, Wyatt couldn't come here right away.

They drove into the night, the silent desert sucking them in after just a few miles, outside of the Paradiso town limit.

Nash flicked on his brights. "Remember, we check for Wyatt's presence first. If he's not there and Brett is, we call off the mission and contact law enforcement."

"And if he is—" Emily placed her hands on her bouncing knees "—we break in silently."

"If he's sleeping, we slip inside the trailer, I'll hold Brett at gunpoint and you'll get Wyatt." He scratched his chin. "I suppose we can't expect Wyatt to be quiet, which means he'll wake up Brett. If this all goes according to plan, you take Wyatt away and call Espinoza. I'll hold Brett for the authorities."

"And we'll take Wyatt home."

"Until DCS sends out another caseworker."

"But this time, Wyatt needs more security. Even with Brett out of the way, there still could be others after Wyatt. He's not safe until we know the whole story."

"I think after the murder of one of their own, DCS will acknowledge the threat and take it seriously."

"Then we're on the same page."

Nash released a long breath. "That's what I like to hear."

The landscape rushed by, the lights illuminating a saguaro cactus here and there, tall enough to resemble a human shape, and occasionally picking out the glowing eyes of some night critter dodging the roaring mechanical intruder into his habitat.

Nash pointed out the mile marker that indicated their proximity to the trailer park. "We're about a half mile out. Any closer and some night owl's going to spot our headlights once we make that bend."

Emily's eyes widened, and the cords stood out in her delicate throat as she swallowed. "We're walking a half a mile in this? In the dark?"

"Thought you were ready." He gave her a playful punch in the arm.

"Oh, I am as long as you're leading the way."

"We can use the flashlights on our phones to make our way down the road. Nobody is going to see those from that distance." He steered the truck into an outlet and cut the engine. As he stepped from the vehicle, the silence of the desert seemed to wrap him in a warm blanket, muffling his senses. He shook it off. He needed all his wits about him.

As if following the desert code, Emily eased her

door shut, closing it with a click. She whispered, "I suppose there are snakes and scorpions out here."

"If we don't bother them, they won't bother us." He touched her arm and she jumped. "Sorry, take my hand and we'll use our flashlights with our other hands."

They stayed on the shoulder of the road, although they could've marched down the center divider as this area didn't have a lot going for it and few people ventured out this way.

Emily stumbled a few times, swore and bumped against him, and then righted herself. After several yards, they got into a rhythm and traversed the distance smoothly.

He put his lips close to her ear as if someone were eavesdropping. "Let's cut our lights. Those rocks up ahead mark the entrance."

"How do you know this place?"

"I've made an arrest or two here."

"Great, so you're not exactly going to be popular."

"Nope, but as we have no clue which ramshackle trailer belonged to Brett's stepfather, we're going to have to check out every one of them until we find him."

"Ugh, I hope nobody's awake." She killed her light and tapped his phone. "Turn your phone off or put it on silent so it doesn't start ringing or buzzing in the middle of the site."

"Glad someone's thinking clearly." He silenced his phone and pocketed it. "Some of these residents may not be outside waiting for us, but my guess is there will be a few of them awake inside their trailers."

He drew his weapon from his shoulder holster and

held it pressed against his leg. "You follow me. I don't want you going off on your own."

"That's ridiculous, Nash. We can cover more ground if both of us are looking." She unzipped the pocket of her purse concealing her gun and pulled it out. "I'm a cop, remember? That's what you keep telling me. Now act like you believe it."

"All right." Yeah, he should've never slept with her. "If you run into any trouble, you scream, yell, shoot your gun in the air. Got it? Don't try to be a hero."

"Same goes for you." She smacked his backside with the palm of her hand.

Hunched over, creeping on silent feet, they approached the boulders. Nash squeezed her shoulder and pointed with his gun to the right.

He watched as the darkness enveloped her, and then he veered left.

When he got to the first trailer, he peered through an open window on the side. A fan whirred inside and light from a tablet cast a blue glow over the interior. When his eyes adjusted, he made out a man and a woman on a double futon. The man's long, gray braid snaked over the edge.

Nash slipped away from the trailer and approached the next one about twenty feet away. Voices carried out the open window of this trailer, and he listened for a few minutes to two women arguing in low tones about the excessive alcohol use of one of them.

Nash backed away from the trailer, feeling like an eavesdropper. As he loped toward the next domicile, an old motor home with no wheels, the hair on his arms prickled. He froze and lifted his head, his nostrils quivering like a horse's.

His ears strained to catch the sound he thought he'd heard—a gasp that hung on the air and swirled right through him. He made a half turn and almost stumbled over Emily.

She looked up at him and put her finger to her lips. She tugged on his arm, half dragging him across the open space of the trailer park.

When they approached a trailer at the edge of the site, she thrust out a finger. She plucked at his sleeve and he bent his head to hers.

"That's his place. I recognize the shoes he left out front." She patted her chest. "He made it easy for us."

Nash slipped a knife from a holster on his leg and placed one foot on the porch. He pressed down on the door handle, and it turned.

He nudged Emily. Brett had made it really easy for them by not even locking his door.

Nash yanked on the aluminum door, and it opened with a huff.

Behind him, Emily had her weapon ready.

He eased open the door and stumbled back, gagging. He held out his arm to stop Emily, but she squeezed past him and fell to her knees.

She cranked her head around, her eyes wide above the hand clapped over her mouth. Her muffled words added another element of horror to the scene.

"He's dead."

Chapter Fifteen

An adrenaline rush spiked through Emily's body, and she crawled past Brett's inert form on the floor of the trailer. She lunged toward a basket next to an unmade bed and grabbed the sides, staring down into a jumble of blankets, one of Wyatt's pacifiers discarded in the middle.

She grabbed it and spun around. Holding it out to Nash, who'd stepped over Brett's body. "Wyatt was here. Brett *did* kidnap him and now someone else has him. We're too late."

She scrabbled forward on her hands and knees and bunched up Brett's shirt with both hands, avoiding the bloody exit wound on his head. "Where is he, you SOB? Who has him?"

Crouching beside her, Nash placed a hand on her shoulder. "Careful, Emily. Don't disturb the evidence."

She released Brett's shirt and brushed her hands together. "There's not going to be much evidence. They must've used a silencer on the gun or everyone in the compound here would've come running."

"Get on your phone and call 911."

"How are we going to explain our presence here?" She pulled her phone from her pocket anyway. The sooner the police knew this dirtbag was dead, the sooner they could go after the next suspect—who might not be so willing to keep Wyatt alive.

"*Now* you're asking me that?" Nash glanced at her over his shoulder as his hands moved through Brett's clothing. "Maybe Jaycee mentioned this place to me or—"

"My God. What have you done?"

Emily held her phone out to the man with the long braid, who was pointing an accusatory finger at Nash still hunched over Brett's body, his flashlight giving his face an ancient cast.

"I'm on the phone to 911 now." She rambled off the nature of the emergency and then paused. "Where should I say we are?"

"Let me do it." Nash pushed to his feet, shoving his own phone in his pocket. He took the phone from her and started speaking with the 911 operator.

Emily squeezed past Nash and out to the porch, where the man with the braid was now throwing up over the side. She took several steps away from him and gulped in some fresh air to replace the fetid odor from the trailer.

When the man had wiped his mouth and straightened up, she called to him, "Are you okay?"

"What happened in there?"

"Someone shot Brett in the head, killed him." She added that last part needlessly. "He was wanted for questioning in a murder and kidnapping. Did you see him with a baby?"

The man narrowed his eyes so that they glittered in the dark like one of those night creatures they'd passed on their way here. "We saw the baby. My wife helped him with the little one. He didn't know what he was doing."

"Yeah, because he kidnapped him." Emily clamped a hand on her hip. "Didn't you know he was wanted? Didn't you see his picture on TV?"

The man shrugged. "People come and people go."

Emily clenched her jaw. No wonder Brett knew he'd be safe here—no questions asked, no police.

A few other people wandered from their trailers and motor homes. A woman called out, "What happened, Zeke?"

The Native American, presumably Zeke, spit into the dirt. "That smell left a taste in my mouth."

"That's death."

Zeke nodded to her and turned to answer questions from the residents. A few broke past him and approached Brett's trailer.

Emily took a step forward. "You need to stay back. That's a crime scene. You don't wanna go in there anyway. Trust me."

A man with a buzz cut and bad teeth leered at her. "Trust you? Why should we trust you? Are you a cop?"

Emily almost smiled at the question. *Depends on who you ask.*

But there *was* a cop on the scene. Where the hell was Nash and what the hell was he doing in there?

"She's not, but I am." Nash emerged from the trailer, large and in charge. "Border Patrol, and this man was wanted by the police for questioning in a murder and kidnapping. Why didn't one of you fine citizens call the police?"

"The police? Border Patrol?" The skinhead blew his nose into the dirt. "We don't like your kind around here."

Nash deliberately walked between her and the skinhead, creating a barrier between them, looming over the smaller man.

"Skeeter, give it a rest." Zeke grabbed a handful of Skeeter's grimy shirt and pulled him back. "They already called 911. I heard them. So, if you don't want to be around when the cops get here, I suggest you go back to your domiciles or head out for a while."

The residents grumbled, but several left the scene, including Skeeter, and a few minutes later a couple of motorcycles revved up and took off.

Emily cupped the pacifier between her hands and rested her chin on the tips of her fingers. "When are they going to get here?"

"A patrol car's on the way. It'll take another thirty to forty minutes for Espinoza and the Pima County Sheriff's Department to get out here." Nash circled her wrists with his long fingers. "Are you okay?"

She closed her eyes for a second. "Pretty gruesome in there, but the worst was seeing that empty makeshift crib. At least Brett wanted to keep Wyatt alive for some reason. What do the others want with him?"

"Again, the fact that we didn't find Wyatt dead in

that trailer next to Brett is a good sign. Brett didn't kill Wyatt when he shot Alice because the baby served a greater purpose for him. The same applies here."

"Excuse me."

Emily turned toward the soft voice. An older woman with short gray hair and a sleeve of tattoos raised her hand and waved. She'd been standing next to Zeke.

"Yes?" Emily raised her chin. She was done getting attacked here when they were the ones who'd had a dead man in their midst.

The woman tilted her head. "Is the baby okay?"

"You were the one helping Brett with the baby?" Emily pressed a hand to her heart. "The baby's gone. He wasn't in the trailer when we found Brett. Did Brett tell you anything about the baby?"

"Thank the Goddess the baby wasn't hurt." The woman crossed her hands over her chest. "Brett told me the baby was his son and that the baby's mother had died in an accident and they were separated at the time, so he hadn't spent much time with Wyatt."

"The baby's mother was murdered, Brett is a suspect in that murder and we're not even sure he's the baby's father. What's your name?"

"I'm Luna. I didn't believe his story, but out here…"

"I know. People come and people go." Emily thrust out her hand. "I'm Emily. Thanks for helping out with Wyatt. Brett kidnapped him from a DCS caseworker after shooting her."

Luna closed her eyes and pressed her fingers against her temples. "He brought violence and discord with

him. I keep telling Zeke we need to move to another location. There's a rough element infiltrating our place."

"Did you see Brett with anyone? Did he tell you anything about someone wanting the baby?"

"He didn't. I'm sorry, but at least the baby is missing
instead of dead in that trailer. I had such a foreboding
when I followed Zeke outside. I just knew the trouble
involved Brett and that little baby. Such a precious little
thing—an old soul. I could see it in his eyes."

Emily blinked. She sensed Nash's restless scorn, but
she understood Luna completely.

Sirens blared in the distance and it took Emily a few
seconds to recognize them for what they were. They
seemed so out of place here.

"I know you folks aren't fond of the police out here
but if you cooperate with the detectives, it might help
bring Wyatt back safely."

"I will do my best." Luna touched Emily's arm. "You
were meant to be with that baby."

Luna floated away and Emily glanced at Nash to
make sure she hadn't dreamed the whole encounter.

His lips twisted. "Earth mother, but at least she's not
hostile like the rest of them."

When the patrol car pulled into the site, bathing the
battered residences with red-and-blue lights, the space
in front of Brett's trailer cleared out, although Zeke and
Luna stood firm.

When the officer exited his vehicle, Nash introduced
himself and flashed his badge. Emily stayed outside as
Nash led the officer to the trailer. They came out sec-

onds later, the young cop covering his nose and mouth with one hand.

Brett's body couldn't have been there that long, but the heat had accelerated the decomposition process and anyone who'd entered that trailer would be living with the smell for a while.

The officer unfurled the yellow crime scene tape and blocked off the area. Then, notebook in hand, he began to question Zeke and Luna.

They had to wait almost another hour for the Pima County Sheriff's homicide squad, led by Detective Espinoza.

When he strode up to the scene, his cowboy hat creating a big shadow behind him, he nodded once to Nash, not looking at all surprised to see him here.

Several minutes later, Espinoza questioned Emily, and she stuck to their story as closely as possible. She assured him that she and Nash would've called the police, but they didn't really consider this a lead—just an offhand comment by Jaycee to Nash had led them here.

While Espinoza turned to ask Nash some further questions, Luna tugged on Emily's arm. "Come to our place for a cup of tea. We'll sit outside so you can keep an eye on things. I have a blend that'll cleanse the evil aura for you."

"I need that." Emily poked Nash in the side and pointed to Luna.

She followed the older woman to her mobile home, where two chairs sat beneath an awning and a tin of water boiled on the camp stove.

When the tea was ready and steeped, Emily sipped

the fragrant brew and tilted her head back to take in the stars, sitting in companionable silence with Luna.

After about thirty minutes, Nash ambled over. "Are you ready?"

"I am." Emily patted Luna's arm. "Thanks for the tea and the company."

As Emily handed the empty cup to Luna, the older woman covered her hand and leaned forward, almost touching her nose to Emily's. "Find that baby."

Nash took Emily's hand and led her back to the police presence. "Sorry I couldn't rescue you sooner."

"Actually, that was just what I needed." She patted her stomach. "That tea had a calming effect. Why are we going back to Brett's trailer?" Emily scuffed her feet in the dirt.

"We're not. Officer Soltis is giving us a ride back to my truck in his squad car."

"Did they find anything? Any clues?"

"None that they shared with me."

"That's it, isn't it? They're not going to share anything with us."

"Shh." Nash squeezed her hand as Officer Soltis trudged toward them.

She and Nash scooted into the back seat of the squad car while Soltis got behind the wheel. "Sorry you both have to ride in back. It's policy."

"Understood, Officer." Nash rapped a knuckle on the wire screen separating back from front. "Thanks for the ride."

A few minutes later, Officer Soltis dropped them off at Nash's truck, and Nash swung his pack into the back seat. Before taking the wheel, he pulled two phones from his pocket, dropped one on the console and powered up the other.

Emily wrinkled her nose and picked up the other phone. "What's this?"

"That—" Nash turned the ignition "—is Brett's phone that I took from his pocket before the police got there."

Her jaw dropped as she clapped the phone to her chest. "Is that what you were doing in there all that time?"

"I figured once Detective Espinoza arrived on the scene, he'd make everything off-limits to us. So, I took a few liberties." He lifted his shoulders. "We can always give it back and say we took it in the shock and confusion."

"You did that for me, didn't you?" She tapped the phone to wake it up. "I know you never would've taken those…liberties if I hadn't harassed you about leaving Wyatt with DCS."

"Maybe, maybe not. Seemed like the thing to do at the time."

"The battery will be dead in seconds." She picked up a charger plugged into a port in the truck and held it up to her face, squinting at it in the dark cab. "This'll work."

Once she'd plugged in Brett's phone, she folded her hands in her lap, around Wyatt's pacifier. "I'm so scared for Wyatt. Why is that baby so important? Whoever took him can't possibly believe Wyatt is Brett's son, right? Brett is now dead. If those two thugs who were looking for Brett found him and killed him, what interest could they have in Wyatt? They presumably got what they wanted."

"Let's look at the other possibility. Wyatt is Lanier's son and Brett was telling the truth—Jaycee and then Brett were looking to blackmail Lanier with this knowledge."

"I can't believe I ever trusted that man…took money from him." She leaned her head against the window and bumped it against the glass once. "But if that's the case, Lanier's in the clear with both Jaycee and Brett dead. Why would he need Wyatt? Nobody else is going to blackmail him. Nobody else needs to know Wyatt is his son."

"I don't know what the guy is thinking." Nash poked at the phone charging in the cup holder. "Maybe he told Brett. I think his phone is sufficiently juiced."

Emily pinched the phone between her fingers and tapped it. "We lucked out. He doesn't have a password."

"Check his texts first."

Emily touched her fingertip to the message icon and scanned the sparse numbers. "This must be a burner phone, like Jaycee's was. None of these messages have names associated with them, just numbers, and he has no contacts stored."

"Probably why he didn't bother with a password. Can you figure out who he's texting?"

"He doesn't have many messages and not a lot of history. Either it's a new phone or he's been deleting them." She swiped at a few of the messages. "These texts are pretty cryptic—nothing like 'Let's blackmail Lanier' or 'I'll meet you at the border.'"

"Damn. Thought I'd hit the jackpot with that phone."

"It was a good idea." She tapped the photos, but apparently Brett hadn't been interested in taking any pictures of *his* son. She scanned a few of the standard apps on the phone, her gaze tripping across an unfamiliar icon with footsteps on a blue background.

She opened the app, which launched a map with a red dot positioned on it. With her fingertips buzzing and her heart racing, she enlarged the map on the phone.

She squealed and twisted in her seat, shoving the phone in Nash's face.

He jerked the steering wheel. "Whoa! I'm driving here."

"You did hit the jackpot, Nash. I know exactly where Wyatt is."

Chapter Sixteen

Nash gave Emily a quick glance from the corner of his eye. She'd taken Luna's hippie-dippie, new age pronouncements a little too seriously. "What, you're communing with Wyatt now and he's sending you his location through the airwaves?"

She poked him in the arm with the phone...hard. "Look at my face. Would I be this excited without good, logical reason?"

He peeled his gaze from the dark road ahead and shifted it to her face for a peek at her glowing eyes and smile that practically reached from ear to ear. "You're serious. What did you find on that phone? A clue?"

"Better than a clue. Remember how Brett tracked us to Tombstone?"

"Jaycee had put a GPS tracker on Wyatt's car seat." His fingers flexed on the steering wheel. "But we removed it and Wyatt's not even in the same car seat."

She tapped her head. "You're a little slow tonight, Dillon. I'll put it down to the late hour and the desert driving. Brett obviously thought that was a good idea because he put another tracker on the car seat from DCS."

"You're sure?"

"He has an app on his phone. It's live and it's tracking something heading up north to Phoenix."

"Something." His heart slowed its thudding. "How do you know it's Wyatt's car seat or even Wyatt?"

She twisted her mouth and studied the phone's display. "What else would he be tracking? He used it to find us in Tombstone, and it must've given him the idea to do it again in case someone grabbed Wyatt—he just didn't figure he'd be too dead to make use of it."

"Okay, that makes sense. If the GPS is attached to the car seat, we can lose Wyatt as soon as whoever has him switches car seats." He wagged his finger at the phone. "Can you tell where he is in Phoenix?"

"You mean, can I tell if he's at Lanier's home or office?"

"Exactly."

"He's not at Lanier's office, at least not the one I went to. I'd have to look up his home address to see if he's there, but if he knows the Pima County Sheriffs are looking to talk to him, I doubt he's going to have Wyatt at his home."

"Espinoza said Lanier was out of the country. I wonder if that's even true. He could've had his office lie for him, or he lied to his office."

"But why, why, why?" Emily pounded a fist on her knee with every why. "He could let it all go right now. I'm certainly not going to suggest DCS do a paternity test on Lanier. I don't care whether or not he's Wyatt's father, and I'm certainly not interested in blackmailing him."

"Does he know that?"

"What do you mean?" She tucked her hands between her knees. "You think he sees me as a blackmail threat? He wouldn't have hired me in the first place if he thought that."

"When he hired you, it was under false pretenses. The way he's acted the past few days by not contacting you, he can't keep up the ruse as the concerned father anymore. He realizes by now you're not buying his original motive."

"Your guess is as good as mine. I don't know what he wants—and that worries me." She ran her finger along the edge of the phone in her lap. "But now we know where he has Wyatt."

"We need to tell the police, Emily. We have to give them this information so that they can formally move in on Lanier."

She grabbed the phone, her lifeline to Wyatt, and hugged it to her chest. "We know this GPS tracking app on Brett's phone is significant, but they don't know that. Do you think the police can get a warrant to search any of Lanier's properties in Phoenix based on a red dot on a phone?"

Nash rubbed his jaw. He'd never considered himself a blind rule follower—until he collided with Emily and her "anything goes" approach to policing. No wonder she got fired from the force. She hadn't even told him the full story of how she tried to nab the accomplice of her father's killer, but he could guess how things went down.

"Look, you have a point, but if things don't go the way we plan them to, we could really screw things up for the police if we go in willy-nilly."

"Me, you—" she pointed to herself and then leveled a finger at him "—we don't do things willy-nilly. We're a good team, Nash."

He reached over and ran a hand down the black, stretchy material of the leggings covering her thighs. "I know you want to rush in with guns blazing to save Wyatt, but we could be putting him in more danger."

She pressed the phone against her cheek. "Does this mean we're not driving up to Phoenix right now and zeroing in on this red dot?"

"Oh, I didn't say that. The closer we are to Wyatt, the better, but we have a few things to do first and it doesn't mean we can't get the police started on what they need to do."

"We have to take care of Denali for one thing."

"Kyle and Meg will take him again, but I do want to swing by my house and grab a bag and a few other things."

Emily practically bounced in her seat. "And then it's on to Phoenix…and Wyatt."

"I don't want you to get your hopes too high, Emily. That red dot—" he pointed at the phone clutched in her hand "—could just be the car seat, probably is the car seat. It doesn't mean Lanier, or whoever has Wyatt, is going to keep him in that car seat."

The light died from her eyes, and her fingers curled

even tighter around the phone so that the veins popped out in her wrist. "I know that. I'm trying not to think about it."

"I know, sweets, and I don't want to be the voice of doom and gloom, but I don't want to watch you crash." He thumped his fist against his chest. "That'll rip my heart out."

She covered his clenched knuckles with her hand. "I know, but I have to hold on to something. When my dad was killed, the one thing that kept me going was the belief that I'd track down the guy who could've stopped it. That thought gave me hope, gave me a reason to carry on. I need that now."

The knife that had been embedded in his gut ever since Jaycee's murder twisted a little more. Emily needed Wyatt to feel whole. He couldn't do that for her. If they failed to bring him home safely, what then? She'd forever associate him with that failure.

He lifted her hand to his lips and kissed the soft skin on the back of it.

"Then I guess we'd better find that baby and bring him home."

She nodded and closed her eyes for the rest of the trip back to his place, her tight grip on that phone the only thing that indicated she wasn't sleeping.

The glow of Paradiso arose from the desert floor like an oasis, and Nash adjusted his speed as his truck approached the turnoff.

When he rolled up to a stop sign and put on the brakes, Emily opened her eyes. "Pack, take care of Denali and get moving, right?"

"That's about the order of things. I don't think we should stay at your place in Phoenix, do you? Lanier may be watching your apartment."

"Maybe, but as far as he knows, I'm off the job and I don't have a clue about him."

"Yeah, I wouldn't bank on that. If he'd contacted you in a normal manner, he could get away with that level of cluelessness, but he must know that you think his response was odd."

"Maybe, but I'm not going to play it like that with him ever."

"Still, it may be a good idea to stay in a hotel in Phoenix."

"I agree."

He pulled into his driveway, beating sunrise by at least an hour.

"I hope Denali isn't going crazy."

"Uh-oh, looks like he got out front." Emily powered down her window and called out, "Hey, boy. It's all right. We're back. Don't run off."

The headlights of the truck picked out the dog as he loped across the front of the house, his tongue lolling from his mouth, his mismatched eyes luminescent in the glare.

"How the hell did he make it to the front of the house?" A tickle ran across Nash's flesh as he glanced at the cameras on his house. He hadn't checked his security footage since their trip to the border. He made a grab for the back of Emily's T-shirt. "Hold on, Emily."

His words came too late. She slipped from his grasp

and opened the door of the truck, hopping out onto the driveway, her sneakers crunching the gravel.

Nash clawed at his phone and his gun on the console and burst from the truck. Denali staggered toward him, whimpered and collapsed at his feet.

"Emily!" His gun now cocked and ready, Nash vaulted over the dog and charged toward the back of the truck.

A figure moved out of the darkness and a low growl sounded close to his ear. "Drop it, or she dies now."

Two other shapes stepped into the lights from the back of the truck, and a cold fear gripped Nash as he made out a man, one arm wrapped around Emily and a gun to her head.

Chapter Seventeen

Emily wriggled in the man's grasp, but the cold metal of the gun pressed against her temple stopped her in her tracks...along with the look of rage stamped on Nash's face.

"I'm all right. I'm all right, Nash. Just do as he says."

The man who had accosted her at the motel sneered at Nash. "And I say drop your piece and head inside for some civil conversation."

Nash's eyes flashed once before he dangled his gun from his fingers and let it fall to the ground.

The man scooped it up immediately and waved it at Nash. "Everyone inside."

"The dog?" Nash folded his arms and widened his stance.

Emily's heart jumped. What had they done with Denali? He'd been out here running around and then disappeared on the other side of the truck.

"We just sedated him with a tranquilizer. He's not dead." The man nodded to her captor. "Let's move, Danny."

While her guy, Danny, kept the gun on her at the

bottom of the steps, Nash unlocked his front door. The man who now had Nash's weapon prodded him in the back with it, and they both walked inside the house.

She knew and Nash knew, one aggressive move on Nash's part would result in a bullet in her head.

Danny pushed her toward the porch, and she stumbled, bracing her hand on the top step. She could've easily swung around on this goon and disarmed him, but she had no clue what kind of position Nash was in at this point. She didn't want to get him killed.

Grabbing her T-shirt, he pulled her up and shoved her again.

She ground her teeth together. "I can walk myself. Stop pushing me."

"Danny, *basta*. That's enough."

When Emily walked into the house, her gaze flew to Nash, sitting at the kitchen table, his own gun trained on him, his jaw set in a hard line.

"My name is Gustavo." His mild tone made it sound like he were visiting for lunch instead of holding them at gunpoint. With his other hand, he pointed to the chair next to Nash's. "Sit down. We just want answers. Nobody needs to get hurt."

"Yeah, like Jaycee? Like Brett?" Emily plopped down in the kitchen chair. "What do you want now? Both of them are dead. Weren't you after Brett all along? Well, you got him."

"We didn't want that skinny junkie dead...or we didn't care one way or the other." Gustavo narrowed his dark eyes. "He took drugs and money from us, hijacked one of our mules just coming across the border."

Nash ground out between his teeth, "And you were willing to use a baby to get him to turn over your property."

"We use what's at our disposal, Agent Dillon, just like you do."

Nash snorted. "So, what? You killed the poor bastard when you found out he didn't have your product? What did you do with the baby?"

Emily held her breath and curled her feet around the legs of the chair. Of course she and Nash wouldn't let on that they had an app to track Wyatt. These two would never tell them where they'd sent Wyatt.

The man's bushy eyebrows, incongruous paired with his shaved head, slammed over his nose. "The baby is missing?"

Emily said, "Nice try. You killed Brett and took the baby. We know. We were there in that trailer to see your handiwork."

He stroked his chin. "We didn't kill Fillmore, and we didn't take the brat. We figured someone killed him for our stash of drugs, and we thought you could tell us who."

Nash hunched forward, his hands on his knees. "You're telling me you didn't kill Brett Fillmore and take that baby."

"That's exactly what I'm telling you, amigo. We didn't kill the girl, either."

"You would say that." Emily crossed her arms over her chest and stuck out her legs, crossing them at the ankles. "You're talking to a Border Patrol agent—not a good idea to confess to any crimes."

Gustavo lifted his shoulders. "Think what you want. The junkie killed his girl. Maybe he thought she was gonna rat him out. He killed that social worker, too, and took the baby, and then someone killed him, took the baby and our property."

Danny, still pointing a gun at her, cracked a gap-toothed smile and spoke for the first time. "We want our stash and you want that baby. Looks like we're on the same side."

Nash grunted. "That'll be the day. Why would the person who killed Fillmore and stole your drugs take the baby?"

Emily had her own theories, which probably matched Nash's, but neither one was going to blurt out anything in front of these two. The farther they kept away from Wyatt, the better. And the more she and Nash kept them talking and thinking they were all in this together, the better.

Gustavo shook his head. "What is it about that baby? I know why we wanted him, but why did Fillmore want him and why did the people who killed Fillmore take him instead of killing him?"

Emily flinched. "Brett wanted him because he was the baby's father. That's obvious. That's why you wanted him—to force Brett's hand."

"Maybe that baby had more value than we realized." Gustavo renewed his grip on Nash's gun. "That's why you're going to tell us where he is and who took him. We'll find our product in the bargain."

"There is no bargain." Nash reached down and

scratched his ankle. "We don't know who stole your stuff and we don't care. We want to find the baby."

"And that's—" Gustavo tipped his head toward Danny "—where our worlds collide. You're going to look for the baby, and you're going to keep us informed so we can collect what's ours. We'll even let you have the brat."

"You've been smoking too much of your own product if you think I'm going to help a couple of soldiers for Las Moscas recover the drugs they illegally smuggled across the border."

"You'll help us, *Agent* Dillon, because if you don't, we'll kill this *pelirroja*." Danny flipped her hair with the barrel of his gun.

Emily jerked away, and Danny smacked her across the face with the back of his hand—just in case she'd forgotten they were actually on opposite sides of the law. Tears sprang to her eyes, and through her blurry vision she saw Nash scratch his left ankle again—where he'd removed a knife from a holster outside of Brett's trailer.

"Hey!" Nash shouted. "There's no need for that. You're gonna make me think we can't work together. If you're not gonna take care of her, I'm not gonna help you."

A smile stretched Gustavo's lips. "I like where this is going, Agent. We'll keep *la pelirroja* safe and sound while you use your connections to find that baby—and our drugs. You keep one. We'll take the other."

"Don't I get a say in this?" Was Nash's plan to get the thugs to separate the two of them so they could each go one-on-one? She knew without a doubt Nash had something up his sleeve…or rather up his leg.

She studied Danny's dilated pupils. She could take this guy, but not while Gustavo had a gun on Nash.

She continued. "Nash, do you really believe Las Moscas will allow either of us to live after this? You? A Border Patrol agent?"

"We won't allow either of you to live right now if you don't agree to cooperate, so I guess you take your chances." Gustavo nudged Danny. "Get her out to the car."

"He's right, Emily." Nash tapped his left knee. "Think about the baby. They have no use for the baby once they get their drugs. He can't be a witness. We have to trust that they won't harm him."

Okay, that had to be a signal. There was no way Nash would ever tell a member of Las Moscas that he was right.

"Listen to him, *la pelirroja*. We'll keep you comfortable while he locates the baby. Then we'll release you." Gustavo's eye twitched, and Emily knew he was lying, not that she needed an eyebrow to tell her that.

"Go with him, Emily. Do what he says."

Another signal if she ever heard one. It'd be a cold day in hell before she ever did what this scumbag told her to do.

"All right, but what are you going to do to him?" She leveled a finger at Nash. "Don't hurt him."

"Hurt him? He's going to help us. We're going to work out a few things while you wait in the car, and then I'm going to join you and leave him here so he can get to work." Gustavo spread his hands. "Cooperation, *si*?"

Emily stood up suddenly, and the gun flashed in front of her.

Danny said, "You move when I tell you to."

"Got it." She stared into Nash's face. "You do what you have to do. I can take care of myself."

Danny jabbed her in the back with the gun. "Move."

She walked to the front door, her muscles coiled, ready for anything on one word from Nash.

When they stepped onto the porch, she asked in a loud voice, "Where's your car? We didn't see it when we drove up."

"Shut up." He gave her a shove from behind and she tripped.

A low growl reverberated in the air, making the hair on the back of her neck stand up.

Something scrambled from beneath Nash's truck, and Danny took a step back. A white flash barreled toward him, and as Denali sank his teeth into Danny's leg, he screamed and got off a shot.

While he hopped on one leg, Denali attached himself to the other. Emily sprang up, wrapped her arms around Danny's middle and tackled him.

Two shots popped off in the house, but she closed her mind to what might be happening inside.

Danny's arm flailed at his side as he tried to take aim with the gun, which he'd held on to but in an awkward position.

Still on top of him, Emily kneed Danny in the groin

and then lunged for the gun. Their hands twisted into an intricate dance to gain control of the weapon.

She ground her teeth together as the gun began to turn in her direction.

"Hold it, or I'll blow your head off." Nash's voice cut through the life-and-death tension, and the man's body went limp beneath her.

She peeled the gun from his hand and rolled off him, panting in the driveway.

Denali whined and licked her face.

"Nash, are you all right? What happened in there?"

Nash strode toward them, handcuffs clinking as they dangled from his fingers. "When we heard the commotion out here, I made a move for my knife strapped to my leg. I was able to stab Gustavo, get possession of my gun and shoot him. He's dead."

Danny swore, and Denali bared his teeth and stood over him so that the drool from his tongue dripped onto his face.

Emily rose to her hands and knees and then stood up. She held out her hands for the cuffs. "Do you want me to do the honors?"

"Do you remember how?"

"Just like riding a bike." She took the handcuffs from Nash, commanded Danny to roll over and cuffed his hands behind his back. She placed her shoe on his neck. "Stay there."

Nash already had his phone out. "I'm calling the Paradiso PD right now."

"Were you just playing dead, boy?" Emily patted

Denali's head. "You came back to life with a vengeance."

"Is that what happened?" Nash tucked his phone in his pocket. "I heard this idiot scream, but I wasn't sure if you did something to him or he did something to himself."

"Neither case." She scratched Denali behind the ears. "When we came out of the house, Danny pushed me one too many times. Denali must've already come out of his unconscious state and immediately went on the attack. When he did, I saw my chance and *I* went on the attack."

"Good job, both of you." He cupped her face and kissed her cheek, which had started throbbing from the slap she'd received inside the house. "I hope you didn't believe I was ever going to allow them to take you away."

"I didn't believe it for a minute. I always knew you had a plan—you were behaving way too meekly." She touched her fingers to her hot cheek.

"You, too." He tapped his own face. "You need ice for that."

"Those two obviously didn't know anything about—"

"Shh." Nash put a finger to his lips and glanced down at Danny, still prone in the gravel with Denali standing guard.

She flipped the gun around in her hand, crouched beside Danny and cracked him on the back of his head with the butt. He passed out with a grunt. "Now we can talk."

Nash raised his eyebrows. "I can see where you would have problems on a PD with your methods."

"I already figured I'm not cut out to be a cop." She handed the gun to Nash. "They didn't know anything about Lanier."

"Didn't appear to, unless they were keeping that piece of info to themselves. We knew they were after Brett, but we finally learned why. He'd stupidly intercepted one of Las Moscas' mules at the border. Did he really think they'd let him get away with that?"

"Maybe that's why he hatched the blackmailing scheme with Jaycee. He planned to return the drugs to Las Moscas."

"They probably would've never let him live after that—or they'd force him into becoming one of their mules. That's what they do—human fodder." His eyes narrowed as he peered down at Danny. "I'm glad you knocked him out."

"So, Lanier, or whoever works for Lanier, took Wyatt and probably took the drugs, too."

"Lanier isn't doing his own dirty work." He stroked her hair. "Look how he used you."

"I wonder if Lanier knows his flunky stole those drugs." She snapped her fingers. "Maybe we can use that information to get Wyatt. If Lanier's hired killer stole those drugs and didn't tell his boss, he wouldn't want his boss to find out, would he?"

"No, but he wouldn't want his boss to know he helped us find Wyatt, either. And there's one small detail. We don't know who the hit man was."

"Hit man?" Emily snorted. "I think you're elevating the guy's credentials. If the killer stole those drugs, he's probably another junkie like Brett."

For the second time in the past twelve hours, sirens blared through the night.

Denali lifted his head, and his ears quivered.

Nash patted the dog's furry side. "You can go inside, boy. You've done a good job tonight. Wait until I tell Clay."

Emily had transferred Brett's GPS app from his phone to hers, and she dragged her phone out of her back pocket to check on Wyatt…or at least Wyatt's car seat. "Wyatt is still in the same spot. Do we tell the police tonight? Do we tell Espinoza?"

"I think we have to, Emily."

"They don't know Brett's recent history like we do. They won't know the significance of this tracker. They won't have the same urgency."

"Maybe not, so we tell them and then we go to Phoenix ourselves. We're private citizens, or at least in this capacity I am. We don't need a search warrant or probable cause. We can get the jump on this, and Espinoza can come in later and tie things up with a bow."

She pinched his sleeve. "Do you think that's how this is going to end, tied up with a bow?"

"I'll do my damnedest to make sure of it, and I know you will, too." He nodded toward the emergency vehicles pulling into his driveway. "But first things first."

The Paradiso PD flooded the scene, along with Border Patrol. Danny came around just in time to be arrested and loaded into the back of a police car.

Emily finally followed Nash into the house, where Gustavo's body lay in the kitchen, blood spreading out from beneath his facedown body onto Nash's beautiful hardwood floor. She had more sympathy for the floor. She only regretted not witnessing Nash take him out.

The police had plenty of questions for her and Nash, and they had to confiscate Nash's weapon. The Border Patrol put him on leave immediately, which would save him from taking another vacation or personal day to go up to Phoenix.

By the time Espinoza showed up on the scene, the sun was rising and the medical examiner had loaded Gustavo's body in the van.

The only thing left to do was clean that floor.

As Emily went through the questions and the explanations, she kept her phone cupped in her hand and kept checking on that red dot. With Espinoza here, she knew they'd have to turn that information over to him. Would he make light of it? Perhaps it would be to their advantage if he did. Then they'd be free to pursue the leads without being hampered by protocol.

That was what she'd hated most about police work. Proper procedures always hampered true justice.

Emily's heart fluttered as Nash shook Espinoza's hand and drew him close. She glanced down at her phone again and sucked in a breath.

The first contact from Marcus Lanier since she'd told him she was working as Wyatt's nanny. She swept the message open, and a tingle of fear crept up her back as she read the text.

Her head jerked up, and she zeroed in on Nash and Espinoza.

Then she rushed toward them to stop the conversation at any cost.

Chapter Eighteen

Espinoza shifted his toothpick from one side of his mouth to the other. "Do you believe that these Las Moscas soldiers didn't kill Fillmore? I can see them going in there looking for their drugs, and once they figured Fillmore didn't have them, they killed him. Wyatt was already gone because the person or persons who kidnapped him didn't know about any drugs and left Fillmore alive after they took the baby."

Nash followed the path of the toothpick for a few seconds before he answered. "That could be. Every word that comes out of their mouths is suspect."

"They must've really believed you could get a line on Jaycee's baby to risk coming to a Border Patrol agent's house and kidnapping your...friend. Why is that? Why do they think you know where the baby is?"

Nash scratched the scruff on his chin and opened his mouth.

Emily butted her way between the two of them and clung to Nash's arm. "When are they going to be done here, Nash? I'm still a nervous wreck. I just want to get back to Phoenix and forget this whole thing."

Nash snapped his mouth shut and studied Emily's face. She winked at him.

Was he supposed to know what that meant? If she thought he was about to tell Espinoza about the GPS tracker on Wyatt's car seat, she'd interrupted that moment for a reason. One thing he knew for sure was that Emily Lang was no nervous wreck after cracking Danny in the skull with his own gun.

"I think they're ready to wrap it up, right, Detective?"

"We are. Ms. Lang, do you have any idea why these two men thought you and Nash knew who took the baby?"

She turned toward him, her hand at her throat. "I have no idea. If we knew where Wyatt was, we'd tell you right away. Maybe they thought it was some other drug dealer who Nash had in his sights."

"They'd be wrong." Nash folded his arms with Emily's fingers still digging into his bicep and covered her hand with his.

Espinoza clapped his hat onto his head. "We're almost done. We'll question Danny Trujillo, for all the good it'll do. We'll see if it was his gun that shot Fillmore, so that'll be a start. He does have a silencer on it. Damn shame about that baby. Don't get why the lowlife who killed Fillmore didn't just leave the baby there, but thank God we didn't find the baby dead."

Emily closed her eyes and swooned against Nash's shoulder, but Nash didn't think she was faking it this time.

He shook his head at Espinoza, and the detective grimaced and said, "We'll be out of your way."

"I'll be off duty for a few days and maybe out of town, but not far. Call me if you need anything else." Nash held out his hand to Espinoza to hurry him along.

Ten minutes later, only the crime scene tape hanging limply outside and the bloodstained floorboards inside gave any indication that a man had died here and another had been hauled away.

When Nash finally closed the door, Emily pounced on him.

"Oh, my God. I'm so glad you didn't spill the beans about the GPS on Wyatt." She pulled his arm and dragged him to the couch.

"I gathered that. You stopped me just in time. I was about to reveal all. Now tell me why we didn't."

When they sat down, Emily tapped furiously on her phone and crooked her finger at him to have a look at her display.

"Read this. It's from Marcus Lanier."

Nash took the phone from her and read the text message out loud. "'I have the baby safe and sound. All you need to do to get him back is tell that Border Patrol agent to delete the file Webb sent him and forget about its existence. If you involve the police, the baby will disappear. Let me know when this is done and I'll let you know where to pick up the baby.'"

Nash dropped the phone, his blood thumping hot through his veins. "What the hell is this about?"

"D-do you know what file he's referring to? Who's Webb?"

"I know what file he means and Special Agent Bruce Webb is the guy in finance who sent it to me, but how does he know about Webb and that file?" Nash dug a hand through his hair. "The information in that file has the potential to show his connection to Las Moscas and his money-laundering efforts on their behalf."

"You have to do it, Nash. You have to get rid of it so we can get Wyatt back."

He whipped his head around. "Do you trust Lanier? He lied to you from the beginning. Do you really think he'd release Wyatt unharmed if I destroy evidence of his criminal activity?"

Her green eyes widened, and the freckles stood out on her pale cheeks. "What's the alternative? Refuse and send Wyatt to his death?"

"Was that what this was about all along?" Nash clasped his hands behind his neck. "It couldn't be. Lanier had no idea Jaycee would leave the baby with me. I doubt he even knew of my existence before this."

Emily held up her hands. "I didn't tell him about you. When I informed him that Jaycee had dropped off the baby with an old friend, I didn't tell him your name or your occupation."

"Why not?"

She lifted and dropped her shoulders quickly. "Just a feeling—a feeling that you were the good guy and Lanier has a lot of money to throw around if he doesn't get his way."

"Well, you got that right." He picked up the phone again and reread the message. "If this opportunity just fell into his lap by coincidence, why was he after Wyatt in the first place?"

"You never did follow through with getting that Rapid DNA test done."

"Like I had time?"

"I'm not criticizing, but what if the story Brett concocted was the actual truth all along? Wyatt is Lanier's baby, but Lanier didn't want that getting out. He didn't want his wife to find out. Or Jaycee was going to blackmail him, so he wanted to…destroy the evidence."

"That could all be true. When Jaycee died, one threat had been eliminated, but Brett knew. He had the baby and he was ready to follow through with Jaycee's plan."

Emily wedged her bare feet on the coffee table and wiggled her toes. "Lanier had Brett killed but, by this time, had figured out who you were and what you could do to him. So when he ordered Brett killed, he also ordered his henchman to take Wyatt as insurance."

"Poor kid." Nash ran a hand beneath his nose. "His whole life he's been nothing more than a bargaining chip."

Emily turned toward him and, taking his face in her hands, said, "That's why we have to rescue him now, Nash. We have to give Lanier what he wants and hope he follows through."

"Listen to yourself." He lightly clinched her wrists. "We're not letting a guy like Lanier get away with his crimes and continue to make money from people's suffering. We're not going to hope that a known liar, thief and killer is going to follow through on his promises."

"I get all of that, but we can't abandon Wyatt." A sob caught in Emily's throat, and tears splashed down her cheeks.

He caught one of her tears with his thumb and sucked it into his mouth. "We're not going to abandon Wyatt. We're going to rescue him without giving Lanier a damned thing except a jail cell in federal prison."

"How are we going to do that?" She swiped a hand across her wet face.

"First of all, I need to find out what Webb knows about all this. How is it Lanier knows the name of the guy responsible for his forensic accounting? Why does Lanier believe he's in the clear once I delete my file?"

"That is weird." Emily scooped up her phone and checked the location of the car seat. "Still there, but with all this work you have to do, we can't get him."

"I want to know what we're walking into." He tapped the phone in her hand. "Lanier didn't mention how we're supposed to know Wyatt is okay. Maybe that's the first thing you text him. Ask for proof that Wyatt is alive and healthy. Tell him I need some time."

"Now?"

"What time did he send that message?"

"Around six this morning—after we took care of Gustavo and Danny." She held her fist out for a bump. "We do make a good team, don't we?"

"I told you. You have the instincts of a cop. Get out of this PI business. You never know what kind of clients you're going to get." He leaned over and kissed the side of her head. "Send that text. I'm going to feed Denali. He deserves a steak."

"Should we take him to the vet today?"

"Does he look like he's suffering any ill effects to

you?" He tipped his head toward Denali in the corner, gnawing on a bone.

Emily cupped the phone in her hand, her thumb hovering over the keyboard display. "What should I write?"

"'We're working on it. Send proof that Wyatt is okay.'"

Her thumb darted over the display, and then she held the phone out to him. "How's this?"

"Hit Send."

Emily sent the text, and Nash went into the kitchen to get Denali's food ready. When he opened the fridge, his gaze tripped across one of Wyatt's bottles, filled with formula. He'd talked a bold game with Emily, but fear clawed at his gut when he thought about Lanier with Wyatt. That man had no regard for the child—whether Wyatt was his or not.

And how was Webb involved in all of this? If Lanier knew Webb's name and title, he must know he had the data, too. He wouldn't put it past Lanier to put a hit on Webb, but the file implicating him would still be on Webb's computer.

Emily called from the great room, "He responded."

"Read it to me." Nash grabbed Denali's dish.

"He said he'd have the woman watching Wyatt live chat with me."

"That's good. Do it now. We have to have proof of life right now."

"I just texted him that."

Denali abandoned his bone when Nash carried his dish out to the dining area. "Here you go. Steak later."

Emily waved her phone at him. "I'm waiting for this person to call me."

Two minutes later, Emily's cell rang and she answered with the phone display toward her.

Nash didn't want to have his mug on this call, so he stood just out of view behind Emily on the couch.

Wyatt's face filled the screen, and Nash swallowed the lump in his throat. The woman didn't allow her own face on the display, but she held Wyatt in her lap and said, "You can see. The baby is fine. He's healthy and well cared for, and Mr. Marcus told me to tell you he'll stay that way until Mr. Marcus gets what he wants."

With a catch in her voice, Emily said, "Hello, Wyatt. I miss you, baby boy."

Wyatt gurgled and smiled when he heard Emily's voice.

Emily blew him a few kisses but then addressed the woman. "What's he paying you? Why would you do this to an innocent baby? Bring him to us, and we'll make sure you walk away from this."

The display swung away from Wyatt and captured a room. A gruff voice came over the phone. "Shut up. The kid's fine. That's what you wanted. Just do what you're supposed to do, and we won't harm him."

Emily shouted, "Let me see him again."

Wyatt appeared on the display again and Emily cooed. "It's okay, Wyatt. We'll see you soon. I love you, baby boy."

They ended the call on the other end, and Emily slumped against the couch cushions.

Nash squeezed her shoulders. "You shouldn't have done that. It didn't help."

"Sure it did." She swung around to face him. "We

know he's not just with some woman. There's a man there for security, and we got to see some of the room where he's being held. There was a window in that room and a view of the outside. I'm going to go frame by frame and enlarge those images to get a better look at everything."

He bent over and kissed her sassy mouth. "You're a badass, Officer Lang."

"I'm terrified that Lanier has Wyatt, but in a way I almost feel better. He won't do anything to Wyatt until he has proof that you deleted his file." She pressed the phone against her heart as if it had captured Wyatt from that chat. "How are you going to contact Webb if you're off duty?"

"Our sector is low-key. Even though I'm on leave, nobody at the station is going to stop me if I want to come in wearing my civvies to close out a little business before taking off. I'll try to reach Webb then. I hope..." Nash bit the inside of his cheek.

Emily finished his sentence. "You hope he's still alive. They couldn't kill him. He still has Lanier's file on his computer."

"That's right, but he only did the investigation into Lanier. He didn't reach any conclusions." Nash wedged his hip against the back of the couch. "If Webb is dead and I delete my file, nobody will pick up the thread."

"Wouldn't you have heard by now if Webb were murdered?"

"If his body has been discovered. What if nobody knows?"

Emily grabbed a pillow from his couch and hugged

it. "I guess you won't know until tomorrow...or rather later this morning when you call him."

"Lanier's communication and that live chat with Wyatt just bought us some time, and I'm going to use mine to get a few hours of shut-eye, a shower and breakfast—in that order. I suggest you do the same."

Emily stared at the red dot on her phone and then held it up. "We have the advantage, don't we? They'll never see us coming."

"We'll hit 'em like a ton of bricks." Nash brushed Emily's hair to the side, like gathering sunset in his hands, and kissed the nape of her neck.

Just like he'd never seen Emily Lang coming. She'd hit him like a ton of bricks...and he'd never be the same.

LATER, AFTER A few hours of sleep with Emily curled up at his side, Nash dropped off Denali at Meg's place. Meg complained that Clay and her cousin, April, should've left the dog with her when they went on their honeymoon, but she just liked complaining.

Nash and Emily went to breakfast, where he wolfed down eggs, bacon, hash browns, toast, the works, while she played with a bowl of oatmeal. He left her with that cold oatmeal and a hot cup of coffee as he made his way into the station.

Valdez blinked when Nash walked in. "You supposed to be here, bro?"

"Does it look like I'm working?" Nash plucked at his white T-shirt and patted his hip. "I don't even have my weapon."

"What the hell went on last night?" Valdez raised his coffee cup as if in a toast. "Brett Fillmore dead. Some Las Moscas soldier dead. Another soldier in custody."

"Baby still missing."

"Yeah, this is complicated. Do you need any help?"

"Nah." Nash pulled out his chair and waved at his computer. "Just wanna close a few loose ends in case the investigation into the shooting takes a long time. It shouldn't, but you already know how slowly the bureaucracy works."

"I sure do." Valdez slurped some coffee. "Let me know if you need anything."

"I will, thanks." Nash waited until Valdez was on the phone, deep into a call. He scrolled through his contacts on his computer and found Webb.

With a sick flip-flop of his stomach, Nash placed the call. He closed his eyes and blew out a breath when Webb answered on the second ring.

"Nash Dillon."

"That's right. Everything okay there, Bruce?"

Bruce responded, "I was expecting your call, Agent Dillon."

Nash's gut twisted again. Hadn't the guy told him the other day to use his first name? Nash licked his lips. Why did he feel that the *Agent Dillon* held some significance?

Nash lowered his voice. "You know about Marcus Lanier and that file, don't you?"

"Marcus who?"

Chapter Nineteen

Nash's hand curled into a fist. Had Lanier gotten to Webb?

He cleared his throat. "The file you sent me linking Lanier's finances to those of Las Moscas—you have it, I have it and Lanier wants it destroyed."

Webb's voice dropped to almost a whisper. "You're the only one who has that file now, Dillon. I suggest you delete it, and I sincerely hope you didn't make any copies or send it to anyone. That file never sees the light of day. I will deny any knowledge of it and its contents."

"What does he have on you, Webb?"

"Just do it, if you know what's good for you and that baby."

"What's to stop me from duplicating the file or not deleting it at all?"

Webb clicked his tongue. "I put in fail-safes, Dillon. You'll send the file I emailed to you back to me. I'll be able to tell if it's been duplicated or attached to an email. Then I will corrupt the file and send proof to our friend."

"He's no friend of mine... Yours, either, Webb. We can do this together."

Webb laughed and Nash knew he'd lost him. The

finance guy who loved numbers had gone over to the dark side.

"He *is* my friend, and while he may never be yours, you don't want him as your enemy. I'll send you instructions on how to embed certain codes in the file. You do that, send it back to me, and he will cooperate with you. Any recording or reporting of this conversation will have a very bad ending for you, Dillon."

He and Emily would have to fix this on their own. "I've been put on leave for a shooting. I won't be back at work for a few days."

"I know that. We have time. I'll explain it to him."

Time. That was what Nash wanted and what Wyatt needed.

"Send those instructions to my personal email."

Webb got Nash's personal email address to send him the instructions to prepare the file for obliteration. He didn't have to know that Nash had no intention of using them—but he would be obliterating Webb's career.

Nash ended the call with a feeling of dread gnawing at his gut. Lanier's tentacles reached farther than he thought, but he didn't know who he was dealing with. When Lanier had hired Emily to spy on Wyatt, he'd unknowingly unleashed a powerful force of reckoning—a mama bear protecting her cub. Emily would go to any lengths to protect Wyatt…and Nash would go to any lengths to protect both of them.

On his way out of the station, Nash waved to Valdez, talking on the phone. He drove back to Emily, still nursing the same cup of coffee.

She half rose from her seat at the booth when he

walked into the restaurant, eyebrows raised in a question—or a hundred questions. She started with two of the most obvious. "Is Webb alive? And if he is, what did he have to say?"

He settled across from her and folded his hands on the wooden tabletop. "He's alive, but he's in league with the devil."

Clinging to the edge of the table, she said, "What does that mean?"

"It means Lanier got to him, and I don't mean in the same way he got to me. Lanier is threatening me. I think he's rewarding Webb."

"Webb's dirty?" She chewed on her bottom lip.

"Yeah, he's dirty." Nash brought his clasped hands to his face, digging his knuckles into his forehead. "My guess is that the guy who loves numbers loves them even more when they appear in his bank account."

Emily whistled. "Does that mean his file on Lanier is already gone?"

"Gone, and he's going to send me instructions to add code to my file so when I email it back to him, he can destroy it."

"Can you copy it first? Send it to me?"

"Webb claims that when I send the file back to him, he'll be able to tell if it's been duplicated or forwarded."

"Do you believe him? That could be a complete lie."

"After the stuff I learned from our IT guy, I don't doubt it. Do you want to take that chance with Wyatt's life?"

"What do you think?" She twisted a strand of hair around her finger. "When are you going to do it, or are you? You seemed to think before that we could have our cake and stuff our faces with it—get Wyatt back and prosecute Lanier."

"I believe that more than ever now." He downed a glass of lukewarm water on the table, probably leftover from his own breakfast. "Webb knows I'm on leave. I can't access the Lanier file while I'm on leave. He's going to pass that information along to Lanier, which buys us time, buys Wyatt time."

She dug her elbows into the table and balanced her chin on her palms. "While Webb and Lanier are waiting for you to get back to work and implant the code to facilitate the destruction of that file, we'll be on our way to Phoenix and Wyatt."

"You—" he tucked her hair behind her ear "—are right."

She spun her phone on the table to face him, and he glanced down at the GPS app that she must've been staring at for the past hour. "Then what are we waiting for?"

"Nightfall, for one. We're not going to charge into some Lanier property in Phoenix to rescue Wyatt in broad daylight."

"We can drive to Phoenix, though. I can't sit around Paradiso knowing Wyatt is with that woman and some guard." She scooped her hands into her hair and grabbed it by the roots. "I'll go crazy."

"With your hair like that, you look a little off balance." He smoothed his hand over her red head. "First, we're going to kill some time by going out to the border and retrieving your rental car."

"I always meant to ask you how you knew I was driving a rental."

He twisted his lips. "C'mon. I ran your plates. You must've taken that into consideration, as the car was rented to Emily O'Brien, not Lang."

"When I rented that car, I didn't even know of your existence. I was creating my identity."

"It wasn't that long ago we met, was it?" He didn't wait for her answer. He didn't want to discuss their relationship right now. "Next, we're going to check you out of that motel."

"Which I barely occupied."

"And we're going to pack a bag of gadgets and disguises and weapons."

She formed her fingers into a pistol and aimed it at him. "Let's not forget the weapons."

They spent the afternoon doing just what Nash planned. When they finally made it out to the border to get Emily's car, they found a smashed windshield.

Emily wedged her hands on her hips as she surveyed the damage. "Gustavo and Danny must've been really upset when they found this car."

"At least Lanier's paying for it, right? What better way to use dirty money than to pay for dirty deeds."

Once they dropped the car off at the rental company, they started packing. The Border Patrol had confiscated Nash's service revolver, but he had his personal stash and he was bringing most of it.

Emily surveyed his weapons duffel bag with an appreciative spark in her green eyes. "Nice collection. You have only two hands, though. Are you gonna share?"

"I've never dated a woman yet who wanted to share—weapons or anything else." He zipped up the bag, closing it to her acquisitive gaze. "But I can be persuaded."

"That's good because I can be persuasive."

"I'm aware of that." He spread his hands to encompass their gear on the floor. "Do you think I'd be doing this otherwise?"

"It has to be this way, Nash. You saw Lanier's warning—no police. And if he compromised some coolheaded accountant, how many others does he have on the inside? I'm sure his close work with law enforcement in Phoenix has netted him a few very good friends in that department."

He held up his hands. "You can stop. You already convinced me."

"You're just giving yourself an out in case things go south." She huffed out a breath. "You never needed any convincing."

He grabbed her around the waist and kissed her hard on the mouth. "But things aren't going south, are they? We're Wyatt Earp and Doc Holliday, and we're gonna make sure justice is served."

EMILY CLAPPED HER hand on her bouncing knee. She could hardly keep still on the almost two-hour drive to Phoenix. They'd missed rush hour, but some freeway construction had made traffic slow.

She stretched out her fingers, which had become cramped wrapped around her phone while she watched the red dot. What if the people who had Wyatt had already moved him to a different car seat, and this pin-point location was for an empty car seat sitting on a trash heap?

Licking her lips, she glanced at Nash, silent and thoughtful behind the wheel and behind his disguise of beard and baseball cap. Was he regretting his decision to go rogue already? She'd been impressed by his thoroughness. When the man went rogue, he went all out.

In addition to his disguise, he'd swapped his truck for a rental in case Lanier's people knew his vehicle. He'd insisted she cover her red hair, so she found a dark wig and did him one better and added a pair of clear glasses.

Sensing her regard, he twisted his head to the side. "You printed out those enlargements of the room where you live chatted with Wyatt, right?"

She jerked her thumb toward the back seat. "I have them in a folder."

He asked, "How close are we now?"

Glancing at her phone, she said, "About twenty minutes straight through the city to the west. It's in the desert, not Phoenix proper. Where are we going to hole up before we make our move?"

"Depends on how close we can get to this location without raising suspicions. If it's in some small town on the outskirts of Phoenix, we'll be strangers. Strangers stick out in small towns. Trust me."

After another ten minutes of driving, Emily got her bearings. "The location isn't in a residential community, but it has to be some kind of house and not a warehouse because it definitely has a window."

"Unless—" Nash grabbed her hand "—we're just tracking an empty car seat."

She threaded her fingers through his. "You don't think that notion has been gnawing at me?"

"We need to drive by the GPS location now, before the sun goes down, and make some kind of assessment. We can't go in blindly at night if we're not even sure Wyatt is with the car seat."

"I agree." She tapped the phone. "We're there in two more exits."

They left the center of Phoenix to where the buildings grew sparser and the desert began to take control again. Emily instructed Nash to turn off where a few fast-food restaurants and chain stores hugged the freeway.

She cleared her throat. "So, not completely isolated. We're not going to cause a commotion with our presence."

Nobody who had seen her or Nash before would recognize them in these disguises, and they'd stashed Wyatt's car seat in the trunk to distance themselves from anything baby related. This could work.

She continued to give Nash directions that took them past a few scattered houses, a trailer park and a rodeo rink. She glanced at Nash from the corner of her eye. "Don't get any ideas."

He snorted, but his mouth stayed firm. He was as worried as she was, and her little joke couldn't snap the tension that held them in its grip.

Emily rapped her knuckle on the window. "Up ahead, the next turn."

Hunching over the steering wheel, Nash said, "Looks like some warehouses, but there could be offices in the front with windows."

"Should we look now, even though it's not as dark as you'd like?"

He nodded. "There are a few cars driving around, probably coming and going from work. One more car isn't going to make a difference. Just keep me going in the right direction."

They turned right into a large lot dotted with warehouses, and Emily's stomach knotted. People worked here. How could they keep a baby tucked away in a warehouse without drawing attention to themselves?

She swallowed. "It has to be this warehouse on the right, Nash, but it looks nothing like what I saw out that window during the video chat."

Nash drove slowly past the warehouse and around the corner. When they reached the back of a gray metal structure, Nash pointed to a sliding door raised a few feet, leaving a gap.

Emily hugged herself. "There's no way they would leave that open if they had a kidnapped baby."

As Nash slowed the car, she grabbed the door handle. "I have to see. I have to see now."

"If he's in there, Emily, you'll give us away." But he'd slowed down the car anyway, and she didn't wait for him to stop.

She jumped out and did a little jog to keep from falling. She crept up to the warehouse door and dropped to her knees, tilting her head to listen. Nash's idling car was the only sound she heard.

She crawled toward the opening and ducked her head into the space. The high windows cast a gray light over the concrete floor of the warehouse, which contained a desk, a few chairs, a filing cabinet...and an empty car seat.

Chapter Twenty

Nash had kept the engine of the car running in case someone came after Emily, but she hadn't moved since she'd crouched in front of that opening to peer into the warehouse.

As he watched her, his heart hammering in his chest, she dropped to the ground, flattening her body against the greasy asphalt.

An animal wailed somewhere, its plaintive cry echoing in the night. It took Nash a few seconds to realize that sound was emanating from Emily.

With the car still idling, he jumped out and launched himself at Emily, who was screaming and kicking her legs against the ground. He scooped her up from behind and cradled her against his chest as he collapsed against the side of the building.

He tried to soothe her by stroking her back. "It's all right. We'll find him. We'll get him back. We'll bring him home. We'll make him ours."

He didn't even know what he was saying. The words tumbled from his lips—all his hopes and dreams stripped bare.

She peeled away from him and pointed at the opening with tears streaming down her face. "It's there, Nash. The car seat—the empty car seat with the GPS we've been following. The GPS we've been pinning all our hopes on."

"Shh, shh." He rocked her back and forth in his arms as if she were Wyatt. "As long as we're here, let's take a look around. Crawl inside and I'll turn off the car."

She followed his suggestion robotically, rolling beneath the door.

Nash jumped up and ran to turn off the engine. Then he slithered into the opening to join Emily. His gut rolled when he saw the car seat in the corner.

He dropped down next to her where she sat on the floor, her legs curled beneath her. Draping his arm around her shoulders, he pulled her close. "Let's look at the positives. He was here. They brought him here and then transferred him to another location."

"Another location that could be anywhere." She bunched his shirt in her hand. "We have to go back, Nash. You have to go back to work and prep that file for deletion."

"Hold on. I'm not ready to admit defeat just yet." He lifted his eyes and scanned the room. "Let's search this building."

Immediately, her head popped up, and she peered into the four corners of the warehouse. "Do you see any security cameras?"

Patting her back, he said, "That's my girl. Get back in the zone."

He pushed off the floor and examined the four corners of the room. "The cameras aren't in any obvious places, and I can't see a space like this having hidden cameras. It's just a storage area."

Emily had crawled toward Wyatt's car seat and buried her face in it.

A few seconds later, just when he thought he'd have to search this warehouse by himself, she withdrew her head from the car seat and sprang to her feet. "You look through those boxes in the corner, and I'll search the desk."

He released a breath. He needed Emily's help, had been counting on it. "Right, Chief."

He strode to the boxes piled in the corner and looked in each one. Most were empty except for a few bits of popcorn packing material. He sniffed inside, but no particular odor hit him over the head.

He kicked the empty boxes he'd checked across the room. "You find anything?"

"Office materials, some invoices that have this address on them."

"Invoices for what?" Nash dived into the next stack of boxes. Address labels. He should check those address labels.

"Parts, mostly. Numbered parts for I don't know what."

Nash turned a box over and checked the label. It listed an address in Buckeye, a small town farther west along the 10 freeway—definitely not Lanier's glitzy Phoenix office building or ritzy home in Scottsdale. Why would he have shipments going to Buckeye?

Emily called across the open space, her voice taking on a slight echo. "Something was written on a pad of paper and left an impression on the sheet below."

"Shade it over with a pen." Nash grabbed the next box and read the same Buckeye address. That address appeared on the next box and the next.

"I got it!" Emily shouted. "It's an address, an address in…"

Nash said it with her. "Buckeye."

"THAT ADDRESS HAS to have some significance, right? Lanier's not going to keep a kidnapped baby at his house or his office." Emily had been chattering non-stop on the hour drive to Buckeye, asking the same questions over and over, coming up with the same justifications.

Nash brushed his knuckles down her arm. "I think we're on the right track. Wyatt may not be at this location, either, but we're on his trail."

She jerked her head up and down. "We surveil the place first to make sure it's not a dead end like the warehouse. If Wyatt's there, we plan our infiltration and carry it out tonight."

"That'll work, and if Wyatt's not there—" he put a finger to her pouting lips "—we glean as much information as we can from that location, as we did from the warehouse. If there are people there, we get the information out of them—one way or another."

"I like the sound of that, Doc."

He managed to grin, despite his stiff face muscles. If they had to hop from place to place in some kind of demented scavenger hunt, he'd have to peel Emily off the floor.

"If you blink, you'll miss Buckeye." She scooted forward in the passenger seat, her phone cupped in her hand. "It's the next exit."

Again, a few stores and restaurants marked the entrance to Buckeye. Signs greeted them for a resort and golf course, an aquatics center, a historical museum and the Gillespie Dam Bridge. They drove past a big-box store and most of the main part of town before it led to the desert landscape.

Nash pulled to the side of the road. "How much farther?"

Glancing at the map on her phone, she said, "Just about five minutes."

"What do you see out there?" He tapped the windshield.

She sucked in her bottom lip and squinted at the wavy desert floor. "Not much."

"Exactly. We can't drive up to *not much* and not expect to be noticed."

"We have to readjust our plan." She dipped her chin to her chest and let out a sigh. "We go in at night just like we planned, but we'll have to assume Wyatt is there—whether he is or not."

He wedged a finger beneath her chin and tilted her head up. "We can do it. If someone is there without Wyatt, they'll never hear us. We'll turn around and sneak back out."

"Then what?" She sniffed but held her unshed tears in check.

"We'll formulate a plan B—we just don't know what that is yet." He pinched her chin. "You on board?"

"I'm on board with you, Nash." She grabbed his hand and kissed his knuckles. "I couldn't do any of this without you. Wouldn't want to. Whatever happens with Wyatt, wherever he winds up—whether that's with you or Jaycee's mother or, God forbid, some other father hiding in the woodwork—you're...my person."

"You mean that?" He laced his fingers with hers. "I'm not just Wyatt's guardian to you?"

He held his breath as she blinked at him. There. He'd put it out there—probably not the best time to do so, but he had to know.

Slowly, she brought their clasped hands to her chest and pressed them against her rapidly beating heart. "Is that what you thought? I know I used you to get close to Wyatt at the beginning and I even understand why you might not trust me after that, but you and Wyatt are not some kind of package deal to me."

He lifted one shoulder. "If I don't adopt Wyatt, there's no reason for you to come around."

"There's every reason—if you'll have me, and I don't know why you would. I'm a failed cop, a hothead, a liar and a kidnapper."

He kissed her hard on the mouth to stop the litany of her faults. He whispered against her lips, "I know all of that, and I still want you. What does that say about me?"

"It says, I must be your person, too." She curled a hand around his neck. "Did you have to know all of that before we went in to rescue Wyatt?"

"Maybe, but it wouldn't have made a difference to my resolve to find that baby and keep him safe—whether that's with me or someone else." He kissed her again. "Let's pass the time until nightfall by getting something to eat and packing the gear we'll need to hike through the desert. We have just a few hours until darkness descends out here and those people in the house or mobile home or tent will never see us coming."

THEY SAT IN a fast-food chain for almost an hour and a half, eating their chicken and drinking refills on their soda. Nobody paid any attention to them.

When they finished, they drove to some bathrooms at the head of a hiking trail, grabbed some bags from the trunk of the car and changed into all-black attire.

Emily removed her fake glasses so they wouldn't reflect any light and give them away under the cover of darkness. She pulled a black cap over her brunette wig, and Nash swapped out his baseball cap for a black beanie.

They each strapped a weapon around their waist, and Nash slipped his knife in the leg holster, which had worked so well in taking down Gustavo.

Emily packed their backpacks with extra guns, smoke bombs, tear gas, burglary tools, GPS devices, small cameras and mics and whatever else she had from her PI stash. "If someone's monitoring the security cameras out here, they might think we're getting ready to take over a small country with this stuff."

Nash cracked a smile. "We have to be ready for anything. We have no idea what we're walking into."

Like their other foray into the desert and the make-shift trailer park, Nash parked the car a half a mile out from where they needed to be. They could see lights in the distance, and he said to Emily, "At least there's more than one house out there."

"Luck is on our side." She rubbed her hands to-gether. "I feel it."

"At least the moon is on our side." He pointed sky-ward at the waxing crescent sliver hanging above them. It kept the night dark.

Emily held Nash's hand and touched her lips to his ear. "At least there's actually a road out here."

"Memorize the location and then shut off your phone. I have a penlight we can use that shuts off quickly—and doesn't ring or buzz."

She studied the display, the blue light highlighting her face, and then shut down her cell and pocketed it. "Got it."

Nash's nostrils twitched. The residents on the out-skirts of Buckeye owned property and horses. He tapped Emily's arm. "I hope Lanier doesn't have horses. They'll sense our presence way before any human could."

She tugged on the strap of his backpack. "That's it."

He gazed across the road at a small house occupy-ing a large lot with one other property behind it, like a mother-in-law quarters. The windows of the house stared out at them blankly, dark and silent, but a soft glow emanated from the small structure behind the main house.

"If they're here, I'm glad they're in the smaller house—easier to storm."

"Don't forget there might be a baby in there." She poked him in the back. "Easy on the storming."

They kept moving past the house and then circled around the side to close in on the cottage with the lights burning.

Nash stuck out a hand and Emily plowed into it, tripping to a stop. He pointed to his eye first and then a pinpoint of light moving up and down outside the front door of the occupied house. "Someone's smoking a cigarette out front."

"The guard?" Emily's breath came out in noisy, short spurts.

They crouched and moved in closer, ducking behind a fence that ringed the front property. Someone had parked a black Jag at a skewed angle in front of the smaller house, and Nash could make out figures moving behind the curtains on the window.

In a low voice, he asked, "Does that look like the window from the video chat?"

"It does. That's it." Emily pulled her gun from the holster around her waist. "He's in there, Nash. I can feel it."

Wrinkling his brow, he said, "What are all these cars? There's a truck around the side, that Jag and a BMW."

"That BMW belongs to Lanier." She tucked her fingers in the back of his waistband. "I'm sure of it. Why would he be out here?"

"And the Jag?"

"I don't have a clue. Seems a little high-end for a bodyguard or a nanny."

"We can't go in with all those people there, and the movement behind the curtain means it's not just the guard who's awake." Nash withdrew his own weapon. His muscles ached with tension.

The guard wouldn't move. As the guy lit another smoke, Nash hunkered down and got comfortable behind the fence post, Emily's quivering body beside his.

They both jumped when the front door of the cottage burst open, and a woman strode outside, her head turned over her shoulder, long, dark hair flying. Her shouting carried through the desert calm.

"I'm sick of it, Marcus. If that kid is yours, we're finished." She jangled a set of keys at the doorway. "No more of your ridiculous stories. How the hell would you be able to kidnap a Border Patrol agent's baby?"

Emily gasped. "Lanier's there. She must be his wife."

"And she's not happy." He pressed his shoulder against hers. "We need to take advantage of this."

Light flooded the front of the house, and a trim, dark-haired man with a distinct widow's peak charged after the woman. "Ming, don't be ridiculous. This opportunity fell into my lap, and I'm going to use it. I don't know anything else about that baby except his father is a Border Patrol agent who thinks he has something on me."

"Thinks?" Ming yanked open the door of the Jag. "I told you to steer clear of Las Moscas. There are easier ways to steal money."

"We have to get in there while they're occupied." Emily shifted away from him and went into a low crouch. "I'm going around the back so I can see who's inside."

"Be careful." Nash placed a hand on her back. "Don't do anything until Ming leaves. You'll hear her car. If Lanier goes after her, we might have a shot."

"We have to take it." Emily blended in with the night as she crept away.

Ming screamed an obscenity at her husband and slammed the car door after her. The Jag peeled away from the house in a cloud of dust.

Nash murmured, "One down. Go after her. C'mon, Lanier. Go after her."

Instead, Lanier turned to the guard and bummed a cigarette from him.

Nash's gaze tracked to the open doorway. Did Emily know Lanier hadn't followed his wife?

Nash dropped to the ground and leveled his weapon in the area of the two men smoking in front of the house. Before Lanier had turned the lights on, Nash couldn't take aim at the guard. Now he raised his weapon as high as he could get it from his position in the dirt. He could probably hit a thigh from here, but then what? He could just make out the bulge in the man's jacket that indicated he had a gun within reach.

And Lanier? A man like that probably never left the house unarmed.

Nash could hit either one, but the other would return gunfire...or worse. Nash didn't know what was going on in the house.

Then Emily decided for him.

A pop sounded from the house and both Lanier and the guard jerked their heads toward the open doorway, the guard reaching for his weapon.

Nash had to go with the man who could do more damage at this point. He jumped to a crouch and pulled the trigger. The report echoed through the night, and the guard fell to his knees, wailing as he clutched his leg, his gun forgotten on the ground beside him.

Nash immediately swung his gun to the left and squeezed off another shot. He missed. Lanier had dived to the ground and was clawing his way back toward the front door.

Could it be Lanier didn't have a gun? Had he even expected to be here?

The guard scrabbled for the weapon he'd dropped in the dirt, and Nash marched forward, leading with his weapon, aiming it at Lanier. On his way, he kicked the gun out of the guard's reach. Then he kicked the guard. Where the hell had Emily gone?

And then like some avenging goddess, Emily appeared in the doorway, both hands clutching a gun, the baby crying in the background.

"Take care of the guard." She aimed her .22 at Lanier, still on his belly. "Stop, or by God I'll shoot you in the dirt."

Nash lunged forward. "Who's behind you in the house, Emily?"

"One dead nanny."

"And Wyatt?"

"Scared but unharmed."

Lanier groaned. "What the hell are you doing here? How'd you know about this place?"

Emily stepped on Lanier's hand. "Does he have a weapon, Nash?"

"If he did, he didn't pull it out. Don't let him out of your sight. I'll take care of this guy."

Nash pocketed the guard's gun and then cuffed him, leaving him on his stomach. Then he rolled Lanier over and winced at the dust covering the man's custom-made suit. That had to hurt. He patted him down.

"He's clean. Can't believe you'd come out to a kidnapping unarmed, Lanier."

"I had no intention of coming out here." He growled. "Someone tipped off my wife."

Nash and Emily exchanged a look, and Emily said, "Not a bad idea, but we didn't think of it."

Not until Nash zip-tied Lanier's hands behind his back did he pull out his phone and dial 911. Once he placed the call, he finally took a breath. "These two aren't going anywhere. Let's see to our boy."

Emily spun around and rushed into the house with Nash hot on her heels.

A woman, the same one from the video chat, was sprawled on the floor, her hand inches from a weapon, blood pooling around her head.

Wyatt, gripping the side of a playpen, his face bright red, screamed when he saw them.

Emily shoved her gun in the waistband of her pants and whipped off her hat and dark wig. "It's all right, Wyatt. It's me. Everything's going to be okay now. You're coming home."

As Emily flashed her red hair, Wyatt blinked and sniffled. His wailing stopped, and he hiccupped once. Then he reached out his arms and babbled, "Mama-mamama."

Epilogue

Emily watched as Nash signed the last form with a flourish.

He shook the pen at her. "Don't get too excited. We still have to wait for the family court date."

She threw herself against his chest anyway. "You're going to be the best father ever."

Nash's fellow agent Clay Archer popped a bottle of champagne while his wife, April, held out the first glass.

April squealed as the bubbly frothed over the side of the glass. "I can't believe our carefree bachelor is going to be a father."

"I wouldn't be able to do it without my live-in nanny."

Clay rescued the glass from his wife and handed it to Emily. "She's not going to be a live-in nanny forever. I talked to my buddy at Tucson PD, and while Emily's previous firing will be a blip on her application, it won't necessarily keep her off the force."

Nash accepted a champagne flute from April. "Are you sure you want to go back to being a cop, Emily?"

"I've practically been a cop the past few days. What are you talking about?" She tossed her fiery locks over one shoulder.

Nash rolled his eyes. "What we did? That was not police work."

"Then I guess Tucson PD has a thing or two to learn from me." She winked at Clay.

"To Nash and Wyatt, father and son." April raised her glass and four rims clinked. Then she took a small sip and said, "Who was it that killed Jaycee? I was so sad to hear the news. That girl never got a break."

"Crazy as it sounds—" Nash sat on a chair at the kitchen table "—with Lanier and the drug cartel guys after her, it was Brett that killed her. The cops discovered evidence that proves it. Apparently, she was pulling back on the idea to blackmail Lanier and Brett wouldn't have it."

"Aw, she wasn't such a bad mom after all." April downed the rest of her champagne, her eyes sparkling with tears.

"You and the underdog." Clay shook his head at his new wife. "So, Lanier is Wyatt's father?"

Emily pressed a hand against her stomach. She didn't want to think that a father could put his baby at risk. "Actually, we're not sure. A paternity test hasn't been ordered yet."

Clay grabbed the champagne bottle by the neck and topped off the four glasses. "Brett killed Jaycee, and Lanier's guy killed Brett?"

Nash answered, "Killed Brett, found the drugs Brett had stolen from Las Moscas and took the baby on

Lanier's orders. By that time, Lanier had discovered that Jaycee left the baby with a Border Patrol agent and had found out that I also happened to be the one who'd received the financial information from Webb."

Clay shook his head. "I can't believe Webb turned like that."

"He'll lose his job, but he did have second thoughts. He's the one who dropped a dime on Lanier to his wife. I'm not sure what he hoped to accomplish by doing that, but her presence at that house in Buckeye is what gave us our chance to rescue Wyatt."

April drew her brows over her nose. "And who was the woman you…killed, Emily?"

"She was part of Lanier's criminal empire. She did whatever he told her to do—and that meant killing Wyatt instead of giving him up." She ran a hand through her hair. "When I broke in the back door of the house, she was going for a weapon."

Nash rapped on the kitchen table. "Emily's been cleared. It was a righteous shooting."

"As was yours." Clay clapped Nash on the shoulder. "It's good to have you back at work."

Denali came to the screen door and barked, and April lunged forward and hugged the husky. "Oh, I missed you, too—especially after I heard how these two treated you, shuttling you back and forth to Meg's, getting you poisoned."

"That dog is a hero." Emily aimed a kiss in Denali's direction.

April tipped her head. "Come out back with me, Clay. I want to dangle my feet in the pool."

"You didn't get enough water in Hawaii?"

April crooked her finger at him.

Clay shrugged, filled up his champagne glass and set the bottle between Nash and Emily on the table. "I think my wife wants me."

As the two of them wandered toward the pool, hand in hand, with Denali at their side, Emily scooted back her chair and sat in Nash's lap. "You're sure you want to take on the responsibility of a baby?"

"I don't have a choice."

Tilting her head, she traced a finger along his jaw. "I thought I told you, you're stuck with me with or without Wyatt."

"I know that." He curled an arm around her waist and drew her close. "While I can't live without you, I also discovered I can't live without Wyatt in my life, either."

She cupped his face with her hands and planted a kiss on his lips. "Are you sure *Paradiso* doesn't mean *Paradise* in Spanish?"

"It has no meaning in Spanish, actually, just some gringo's butchered attempt at naming something in Spanish. Why?"

"Because I came out to Paradiso and found a man, a baby and a love I've never felt before. Seems like paradise to me."

Nash kissed her back and proved her point.

* * * * *

Look for Unraveling Jane Doe, *the next book
in Carol Ericson's Holding the Line miniseries,
available August 2020.*

And don't miss the previous book in the miniseries:
Evasive Action

*Available now wherever
Harlequin Intrigue books are sold!*

"Two cops broke into your house?" He didn't bother to take out the skepticism. "Did they have a warrant? Did they ID themselves?"

Ashlyn shook her head. "They were wearing uniforms, badges and all the gear that cops have. They used a stun gun on me." She rubbed her fingers along the side of her arm, and the trembling got worse. "They took Cora, but I heard them say they were working for you."

Eli's groan was even louder than the one she made. "And you believed them." The look he gave her was as flat as his tone. He didn't spell out to her that she'd been gullible, but he was certain Ashlyn had already picked up on that.

She squeezed her eyes shut a moment. "I panicked. Wasn't thinking straight. As soon as I could move, I jumped in my car and drove straight here."

The drive wouldn't have taken that long since Ashlyn's house was only about ten miles away. She lived on a small ranch on the other side of Longview Ridge that she'd inherited from her grandparents, and she made a living training and boarding horses.

HIEXP0720

"Did the kidnappers make a ransom demand?" he pressed. "Or did they take anything else from your place?"

"No. They only took Cora. Who brought her here?" Ashlyn asked, her head whipping up. "Was it those cops?"

"Fake cops," Eli automatically corrected. "I didn't see who left her on my porch, but they weren't exactly quiet about it. She was probably out here no more than a minute or two before I went to the door and found her."

He paused, worked through the pieces that she'd just given him and it didn't take him long to come to a conclusion. A bad one. These fake cops hadn't hurt the child, hadn't asked for money or taken anything, but they had let Ashlyn believe they worked for him. There had to be a good reason for that. Well, "good" in their minds, anyway.

"This was some kind of sick game?" she asked.

It was looking that way. A game designed to send her after him.

"They wanted me to kill you?" Ashlyn added a moment later.

Before Eli answered that, he wanted to talk to his brother and get backup so he could take Ashlyn and the baby into Longview Ridge. First to the hospital to confirm they were okay and then to the sheriff's office so he could get an official statement from Ashlyn.

"You really had no part in this?" she pressed.

Eli huffed, not bothering to answer that. He took out his phone to make that call to Kellan, but he stopped when he saw the blur of motion on the other side of Ashlyn's car. He lifted his hand to silence her when Ashlyn started to speak, and he kept looking.

Waiting.

Then, he finally saw it. Or rather he saw them. Two men wearing uniforms, and they had guns aimed right at the house.

Don't miss
Settling an Old Score *by Delores Fossen,*
available August 2020 wherever
Harlequin Intrigue books and ebooks are sold.

Harlequin.com

HIEXP0720

Get 4 FREE REWARDS!

We'll send you 2 FREE Books plus 2 FREE Mystery Gifts.

Harlequin Intrigue books are action-packed stories that will keep you on the edge of your seat. Solve the crime and deliver justice at all costs.

FREE
Value Over
$20

What could she tell him? Her situation was horrid.
Frightening. Desperate. And that was why she had to
keep Luke out of it. She had to protect him from the
ugliness that her life had become and the danger Joseph
posed.

But he was standing there, all devastatingly handsome,
earnest and worried about her. She had to tell him
something. The lies she'd told friends for years to hide
the truth tasted all the more sour as they formed on her
tongue, so she discarded them for one that was more
palatable.

"A few years back I made some…poor choices," she
began slowly, picking her words carefully. "And I'm

trying to correct those mistakes. Until I get my life back on track, my finances are going to be tight. But I can't make the fresh start I need if I accept money from you or anyone else. I need to do this by myself. To be truly independent and self-sufficient."

"Poor choices, huh?" A hum rumbled from his throat, and he twisted his lips. "We all make those at some point in our lives, don't we?"

With his gaze still locked on her, he inched his palms from her shoulders to her neck, and his thumbs now reached the bottom edge of her chin. His work-roughened hands were paradoxically gentle. The skimming strokes of his calloused fingers against her skin pooled a honeyed lethargy inside her. Reason told her to pull away, but some competing force inside her rooted her to the spot to bask in the tenderness she'd had far too little of in her adult life.

Luke is the kind of man you should be with, the kind of man you deserve.

Don't miss
In the Rancher's Protection *by Beth Cornelison,*
available July 2020 wherever
Harlequin Romantic Suspense
books and ebooks are sold.

Harlequin.com